STRIK...

A SHORT STORY COLLECTI...

DAPHNE GLAZER

*Daphne
Glazer*

PewterRose
PRESS

PEWTER ROSE PRESS

Published by
Pewter Rose Press
17 Mellors Rd,
West Bridgford
Nottingham, NG2 6EY
United Kingdom
www.pewter-rose-press.com

First published in Great Britain 2014
© Daphne Glazer 2014
ISBN 9781908136411

The right of Daphne Glazer to be identified as author of this work has
been asserted by her in accordance with the Copyright, Designs and
Patents Act 1988

British Library Cataloguing in Publication Data
A catalogue record for this book is available from the British Library

CONTENTS

INTRODUCTION

I have written these stories over several years. Many of them have arisen because of my work as a Quaker Prison Chaplain, which has granted me a view into lives often twisted by appalling social circumstances and emotional neglect, but also nevertheless containing an indestructible core of goodness.

The short story is, I think, the perfect form for capturing moments when a person's intrinsic nature can be shown. In 'Charlie' for instance Dot's overpowering love is for her long-dead husband, never mind the fact that her entire life-savings have just been robbed.

I love too the way a short story reveals, peeling back the moment, so that the reader and the characters must reappraise the situation.

Several of these stories have allowed me to explore areas of imprisonment to which I would normally not have access. I based 'Scents' on a visit I was once able to make to a German prison. There I met a long term female prisoner and at her request corresponded with her for many years. She wrote after she had been on a short term release – a few hours out of prison prior to a possible eventual release – how the experience had been quite overwhelming. I have heard this too from long term male prisoners in this country. I have tried to indicate something of the acute sensory deprivation which very long term prisoners experience.

I hope that you, the reader, will find these stories thought provoking.

For Peter

I would also like to thank:
My daughter, Imogen, for her helpful comments
Margo O'Sullivan for reading and suggestions
Mark Elwood, champion kick-boxer, for stories.

CLOSE ENCOUNTERS

Standing before class the whole day, Poppy has only one picture in her head: David, turning, with a huge suitcase in either hand. His face is quite blank, as though he is already somewhere else. As she pushes her books and files into her back-pack, she cringes at the thought of the silent house. He isn't there… will not be returning later… not ever. It is as though he has died. This morning he was there, and now in a flash he has disappeared and cannot be brought back.

"I've got to say it, Poppy, I don't think we're compatible. I'm just not happy being here. I want to find myself… find who I am."

There was no screaming, raving, wild weeping… no, that is not how she behaves. There was just silence. Poppy has learnt from experience that the expression 'I want to find myself' means 'I want to find someone else.' She cannot argue with this. Perhaps he already has somebody in mind… A stifling heat bubbles up in her chest. What is it? Despair? Hopelessness? Here she is, thirty-three years old, nearly thirty-four, and her newness has worn off; she is no longer seventeen going on eighteen, thrilling with the drama of what lies ahead. All the men she meets have lengthy back-stories. She senses that they contain lots of failures, things that didn't work out. They have grown to expect disasters and their low expectations bring on what they have tried to avoid.

So much to worry about, now there is the hatchet poised above her head: will the school close; will they all end up jobless? The new Head has been sent expressly to fire as many staff as possible, because the LEA don't want the expense of paying out redundancy money.

She is late leaving the school and so sunk in gloom that she almost walks into a body spread-eagled on the pavement. Traffic blasts by on the main road and workers stream out of a nearby factory, but nobody pays any attention to the man on the ground.

A person won't lie flat out on the pavement unless something has happened. Perhaps he has had a heart attack. She stares down at him. Clumps of vomit stick to his jacket, and his trousers are patched with damp. From the smell of him he must be drunk and have wet himself. Lying on his back like that, he is in danger of choking.

She appeals to the workers leaving the factory… have any of them got any plastic gloves? Nobody meets her gaze, as though they are frightened of becoming involved. When she has given up hope of any response from the bystanders and the factory workers, a man hands her a piece of cloth.

"Thank God, he's breathing!" Poppy kneels down and by degrees hauls the man into the recovery position, so that he lies face down with his head turned to one side. The reek coming off him sticks in her nostrils and makes her want to shudder, but she tries to hide her reaction. Before she can phone the police a posse of teenagers saunters up. Poppy thinks some of them used to attend the school.

"Ugh, look at him!" They have stopped near the man, and one pokes him with the tip of his boot. At that the man surfaces from his drunkenness, scrabbles himself upright.

"I'll fuckin' bang you one!" the tramp screeches.

The lads roar with laughter.

"Come on, bang us then!" one of the group yells.

"Or right, or right!" The man gesticulates, tries to rise and falls back.

The lads' jeering intensifies. "Come on, we're waitin' for you!" They jump about, running in near him, making him grab at them and topple sideways.

Poppy is phoning for the police and ambulance, when another drunk lurches up.

"I'll gie you a fuckin' bang," he growls, and kicks the first man, who falls back on the pavers striking his head.

The dull, heavy crunch of flesh and bone hitting stone brings the sickness to her mouth. The man twitches and then lies motionless.

Dear God, Poppy thinks. He's dead. "Get back! Get back!" she shrieks at the youths, who move away, shocked. The second drunk stands staring down at the unconscious man. He is much younger than the injured man, and Poppy sees the dirt ingrained in his hands. He wears heavy boots, jeans, an old jacket and a baseball cap. His skin is grey with dirt and dusted with black heads. Poppy hopes he won't try to escape before the police arrive.

A police van drives up. After that everything streaks along. The victim is stretchered off into an ambulance and the younger chap disappears into the police van. The group of youths vanishes.

Poppy is left to walk to the bus stop. She cannot rid herself of the sound of the man's head hitting the pavers. Why was the man there? What is making him drink himself to death? And the chap in the baseball cap… what were they trying to blot out?

On the top deck Poppy stares down at the people in the street: men smoking or nattering into a phone, entering the supermarket, scurrying women pushing buggies, smaller children running along side, a boy being hauled forward by a dog. Every one of these people holds a story – are the men going to buy cheap booze to consume in lonely rooms?

The harsh smell of vomit and stale urine seems to cling to her clothes and fill her with disgust. She feels her stomach heaving at the odour. She understands the reluctance of others to help her roll the drunken man into the recovery position. Her hands are unclean – she must take care not to touch her face, or any part of her skin until she has washed her fingers in the germ repellent gel that she keeps in the kitchen by the taps. She plans how she will pull off her clothes and sling them into the washing machine, then she will take a long shower.

In the Infirmary they will be washing the tramp... but will he have survived the crash onto the pavers?

If only she could stop hearing the sound of his head cracking. The blow brought a rush of scarlet from his nostrils. The blood and snot trickled down his cheeks. The sight of it focussed the lads' disgust. Ugh! Look at that... fuckin' yuck...discustin'. They drew back, but fascinated, wouldn't shamble away until the police van lumbered up.

She showers, rubs her body with geranium scented soap and washes her hair with moisturizing shampoo but the greyness persists. The horror of the tramp's disintegration; the simple, but revolting details of his body's breaking, merge with the coldness in David's voice as he turned to her... I want to find myself... and now the isolation; the aloneness... not even arguments to mull over. Those two tramps are also alone, locked in some inarticulate desperation.

Even after the shower and the hints of geranium on her hands, she doesn't feel well. It's a long time since she ate anything, but she can't be bothered...

The first thing David always did on entering the house was snap on the telly, but now it is silent. He isn't banging around looking for something he has mislaid. The house feels his absence.

Driven out by the greyness she goes into the garage and backs her car out. She knows where she must go. The decision brings a new calmness. She stops hearing the drunk's head smashing down. Soon she has left her street behind and travels up a dual carriageway. It's June, but blustery, damp and chill, it might have been February or March. Rain has been falling for two days, but today the sky is grey and the wind drives the rain back.

She sees the bridge before her. It soars above the Estuary, but the water over which it arches has been squeezed by the retreating tide until only a dimpling expanse of mud remains. She has often viewed the Humber from a train window, and been dazzled by the frilling gun-metal waves and the glistening pebbles on the shore line. With its many moods it radiates an austere beauty.

This is the static time of day when people are in their houses having a meal, maybe listening to the news on telly or radio, a fallow period before the evening's happenings, and the streets are empty.

Up here by the bridge the wind jerks tree branches and bushes to and fro. She parks her car and makes for the pedestrian walkway. This is where people dive to their deaths. They scale the railings and drop over: an easy way out.

A dark-haired man in a denim jacket leans on the rail. She can see no-one else the length of the span. No cars cross; nobody nearby – just her and the unknown man. He doesn't seem at all prepared to move on. She has drawn level with him, wonders whether to hang back or keep walking. Now close by him, she has the chance to study his back – he doesn't turn. His hair is thick and quite long and he is wearing stone-coloured chinos and trainers. Will he glance round at her? No, he keeps his back towards her. She sees the mud below them like melted chocolate with the water channel squirming down its centre.

She keeps on walking. The wind blasts in her face and slams her hair about her cheeks and across her eyes. Is he still there? What if he jumps? She must go and speak to him. But what on earth can she say? Will I – won't I? The tussle hammers in her head. She begins to stride back. Her heart bobs in her chest as she sweats and freezes.

He hasn't moved – except that he seems to be leaning further over. She almost breaks into a run and hears herself panting.

"Bit breezy," she opens.

He doesn't respond. Perhaps he hasn't heard her, or thinks she is addressing someone else. "Not so good for June is it?" she says. Thank God for the weather, it never fails. He swings round now and looks at her.

"Doesn't seem to be encouraging people to come out, does it?"

"What doesn't?"

Poppy can see that he has no idea what she is talking about. "The weather, it's so cold. I mean, not like June at all."

"Right."

Her cheeks begin to glow and all of her is seized with embarrassment.

What the hell to say next? "You looking for something?"

"No."

"I mean, I saw you before when I first arrived and then I couldn't help noticing."

"And you thought – he's going to jump off?"

The man wears glasses and has a thin, intelligent face like a nervous horse. Her flush deepens until her neck and chest blaze. "I don't know what I thought."

"Or you thought you'd jump off."

She wishes she hasn't started this conversation. But she knows she couldn't have left him... she has to find a way of diverting him from jumping. "No, actually I just wanted to clear my head... not had a good day." She must hold his attention, get him to focus on her. He doesn't appear to be listening. "Now at this point," she says, smiling, "you're supposed to ask me why... give some show of sympathy." She continues to grin and talk as though this person were not a stranger but someone she knows well.

"Why?"

"Because we're the only people up here on this bridge and we need to talk."

"Speak for yourself!"

"Listen, if you could talk more, I bet you wouldn't be up here like this, on your own."

Her hands sweat.

He stares at her.

The silence of the bridge and the grey road stretching between the great supports make her feel dizzy, and the fact that she is talking to this stranger in an almost intimate way.

"So you think you're going to save me?"

"Look," she says, and her insides feel like a blazing bonfire, "I've already seen a chap drunk out of his mind this afternoon in the middle of the town and he hit his head on a paver and may be dead... I've had enough of it, so pack it in! You'd better come with me. I'm not going to save you, you're going to save yourself."

After this thrust of rage, she stands glaring up into the man's face. All of her dithers with the aftermath of emotion.

The man looks shaken, amazed. "All right, all right... what is it?"

"We're going to go to a caff I know on the foreshore."

He turns to her, nods once, and a mood of exhilaration seizes her.

FINDING OUT

Lucy dumps her boots, jacket and backpack in a plastic tray, and watches them slide along a belt into a tunnel. She walks under a metal detector, whilst a gang of officers watch her. Just normal routine. She reclaims her possessions and for the blink of an eye she stares back through the reception doorway at the September morning. The haze will burn off later and give way to a misty golden day. She wants to turn round, escape to her car and drive home. But she doesn't.

Waiting for the electronic door to open, she returns to yesterday evening's scene with Simon.

"What's wrong?" he said. He never likes it when she goes quiet – she must have been a bit short with him.

"Oh, just thinking about Monday…"

"Well, Luce, for heaven's sake, you don't have to work there. If you don't like it, quit… I mean, it's not very pleasant for me living with someone who's always moaning on."

"I'm not always moaning on."

Voices rose. She tried to explain. It's just that I put a lot of effort into things – I'll think somebody's going to do well, and then they get moved on, or he says he's fed up and wants to give up… and you never know what's going to happen next. It's like working for nothing.

"Leave the blessed job – I can't imagine why you do it. Teach in a school."

He was irritated, bored with her problems. Perhaps he's right, perhaps she should pack her job in. She has never told him how she's often scared because the whole place is spooky and there are warnings: security briefings about not pressing alarm buttons or screaming if you're taken hostage because you might cause people to get killed.

As she unlocks and locks doors, passes through electronically controlled areas and along subterranean, windowless corridors, she thinks of Dave Ford – like the others in the class he's an unknown quantity, only more so. When he first arrived, she was told, "Watch him, he's very violent, he's a lifer – in his last nick he assaulted a teacher and even the governor – he's very dangerous. You don't have to teach him if you don't want to." But of course it would not have been politic to refuse, and so she smiled as usual, said of course she'd teach him.

At the sight of this hulk swaggering into the classroom, she was on her guard and has been ever since and wonders how long he'll last. They said he'd be moved on pretty fast because he foments trouble wherever he goes and has spent a lot of time in solitary confinement.

Without the fear of what Dave might do, things would jog along reasonably. Phil gabbles non-stop and his blue eyes burst out of his skull with hyperactivity, he's irritating but harmless. Andy is equally voluble. The older man, Ken, very red in the face and affable-seeming can crack out in unexpected tetchiness. Al is the quiet one, a non-talker. Several more chaps come and go but they're polite and can be quite pleasant.

She thinks back to her first day with Dave. Right from the start he was going to show her. He sat at the opposite end of the table from her and glowered. When she explained about the GCSE English assignment, Personal Writing, he said, "I'm not writing about my life – no way. You aren't going to get me to tell you no tales, no that's my business – keep that out!" And he tapped the side of his nose and narrowed his eyes. He wanted to force her to launch into head-on conflict. She struggled with irritation but managed to suppress it and keep smiling.

"That's all right, you can make up a life, can't you? Have some fun dreaming one up."

"But I thought it had to be true."

The others were listening in. Dave would soon have them stirred up.

"Well, not necessarily. I suppose whoever set the syllabus probably thought people would find it easier to write about what they know."

"Yer right," he said – but he didn't write anything and straight away Phil started up how he couldn't write about his childhood because it made him feel depressed. So she had to Mummy him along whilst wanting to throttle him.

The only one who never causes trouble is Al. He sits and writes intense things which are difficult to understand. Throughout all potentially difficult situations he keeps his head down and takes no part.

On reaching the staffroom she unpacks her files and the creative writing pieces she marked after the exchange of words with Simon the previous evening. She hears her voice saying, "Imagine that somebody receives a letter and when he opens it, his whole life is changed by the contents."

Dave's work lies before her. She feels compelled to reread it.

John and Ellie grew up in care. At first they fought. She was a tough kid and liked her own way, so did he, but then they became lovers like you've never seen.

9

When they got out, they went robbing together like Bonnie and Clyde. They always knew they would never be separated, but he got a twelve stretch for robbing a bank. She didn't come on visits and he couldn't understand that. Then he got a letter from a friend telling him Ellie had died of an overdose. After that he didn't care no more, but he thought of her, he thought of her all the time because they were part of each other.

She wishes now she hasn't re-read Dave's story. It has returned her to Simon and last night's argument. Simon won't feel he has lost half himself, if she died suddenly. All right he might be depressed for a few weeks but then he'd find someone else and forget. He could never write 'they were lovers like you've never seen.' They've lived together for five years now and he's fine as long as she smiles and doesn't argue. Weakness seems to irritate him. He has to have emotional matters neat and tidy, no mess, but then he is an accountant and they have to balance the books.

Colleagues bluster in lugging briefcases and plastic bags and the air rustles with conversations about the past weekend and locker doors rattle shut, keys turn. Lucy tries not to think of that sudden coldness; that view into her own life. She makes a joke with the art teacher and heads off to the classroom with the pile of corrected stories.

She sits down at the top of two long tables that have been pushed together and stares through the key patterned bars, waiting for the men to be brought from their cells. Outside a dog handler stalks by with a huge hairy beast leashed in at his heel. Day and night they patrol along by the electrified fence. Far off a dog howls. In the room the air is clammy and she shivers.

Dave arrives first.

"Morning," she says, "I thought your story was very moving."

In answer he drops some A4 sheets of paper on the table before her. He doesn't explain anything and goes to sit down. She chances a glance at his face. He worries her. Two weeks ago he didn't appear in class and the others said he'd heard his brother had been murdered. Since his reappearance he has been very quiet. She looks down at the A4 sheet and finds herself reading.

My Dad was a seaman, came from West Africa – I got eight brothers and sisters most brown as conkers but me pink. My life of crime started when I was six. My mam went to get some electric meter tokens because the electric had ran out – while she was gone, this social woman came a noseying and she finds us kids on us own. It was bang, kids' home for us. They said my Mam was an unsuitable mother. I hated this kids' home and I runs away. I did that a lot. I was in care until I was sixteen.

They broke my arm in care. By thirteen I carried a gun.

She reads on, a tale of abuse, beatings, killings. The group trundles in by degrees and the plastic chairs squeak on the vinyl floor tiles as they barge into them or flop down at the table.

"I really enjoyed your stories," she tells them, "and I'll see you individually about them in a minute."

Her gaze turns to the day beyond the bars. The sky is a grey bolster pressing down, scrawled by the electrified fence and the razor wire. The sun has vanished. Dave's life story and Simon's irritation jangle in her head. She makes an effort and launches into the new topic: description of an industrial landscape. When she's finished explaining, Phil says, "I don't know what you mean. What is it you want us to do?"

"She told you, mega mouth," Andy says.

"Don't mega mouth me," Phil spits.

"You never listen – she's told you what to do."

"Oh yer, teacher's pet – apple for the teacher."

Lucy intervenes with soothing words, in an attempt to ease the lesson back on course.

"I don't know what industrial landscape is."

"Yer, because you never listened – you never do, you open your big gob first."

Phil and Andy glare at each other. She explains the assignment once more. The uneasy ripples in the atmosphere have put her on edge but she tries to dismiss them.

Some have started writing. Lucy is staggered to see Al leap to his feet. The table judders. Al's chalk-white face convulses in rage. Somehow everything has sped up. She's drowning, feels as though her head has plunged under a great wave. She fights for breath. Her heart clatters around her rib cage. Al fists Andy. Chairs topple over, limbs flail. She hears them panting and snorting and kicking out. Staggering up from her chair she mumbles something half strangled like, "Please – that will do." She tries to get in between them and receives a slap across the face from Al. She gasps with pain and shock.

And then it all stops. She sees Dave wrenching Andy and Al apart. The others sit gawping. Phil has backed off anyway.

"Okay, cool it man," Dave says, turning to Al, who looks shocked. The scene has probably only lasted a few seconds but Lucy has the sensation of it having gone on for hours. Her face stings and her head throbs and she wants to cry.

"I think," she manages to say, "we ought to have a break now. Thank you for that," she says to Dave as he is leaving.

"You all right?" he says smiling at her.

"Just about," she says, returning his smile.

In the staff room whilst she's making a mug of tea and preparing to write an incident report about the scene in the classroom, she tries to digest what has just happened: Dave, the notoriously dangerous man, has saved her. And she… why didn't she press the security alarm, but went instead to try to separate the combatants? The day is irradiated by miraculousness, and she has found herself, in some amazing way, released – as though by moving into the heart of her fear she has conquered it.

The rest of the day slides by without event and she leaves the prison at 4:45, still enveloped by this feeling. Exhilarated. She sets off on the hour-long drive home.

For once she feels strong. September, time for a change. Things are going to be different, and whatever will happen, she will meet it.

She looks at the banana-fingered sycamore leaves somersaulting down to lie in ochre drifts and the last brilliant splurges of purple and shell-pink petunias in hanging baskets and gardens, and she sings as loud as she can and taps the steering wheel.

PUTTING OUT TO SEA

Julie-Anne must tell them tonight. If she fails to, she may never have the courage.

It is only late September but wind slams on the windowpanes. It sounds like waves pounding or swilling against stone. Trawlers out on the North Sea will be listing and rearing. When all the male members of your family have been to sea, just like their fathers, it becomes second nature to think of it.

The beating of the wind swings her into the far past. She was ten – the end of the summer holidays and she already heard the rumble of her insides with school sickness. You must play all the harder, eke out the last zizzy of excitement to stave off the inevitable. Wind blasted in off the estuary and brought Julie-Anne and mate, Sharon, down from Julie-Anne's bedroom where they'd been listening to CDs and exchanging secrets. They stampeded into the kitchen to raid the fridge but Julie-Anne halted before the window and gasped. The backyard was crammed with a boat, a big curvy boat. Sharon's eyes grew round as gob-stoppers. They pelted out, fridge forgotten.

In a second they scaled its broad sides and began to rock. To and fro the boat lurched and the wind snagged their hair. The craft bucked and toppled on seas that curled up as high as houses and swung down into troughs deep as lead mines. Screeching with laughter and terror they rocked and the boat juddered with a mind of its own.

"We're going to die!" Sharon yelled. "We'll drown."

And Julie-Anne already felt the water in her lungs choking her. The boat was capsizing.

"Stop!" bellowed her mother at the back door.

Later that night from her bedroom she heard the raised voices. Uncle Alan, her dad's youngest brother, two more uncles and her dad filled the kitchen. She loved Uncle Alan as much as her dad. He wore a single thick gold earring and his cheeks were sandpapery and he would rub them against her to make her scream in mock terror. The scar under his left eye fascinated her. He looked like a great blond 'Scrob'. But now she understands what drew her most to Alan: he wouldn't be pulled into line, he was a wild one.

She remembers those voices downstairs in that little brick terrace, now demolished by the council. You could hear every sound in it, even

13

the flushing of next door's toilet. Her dad's voice was loudest – being the eldest he led the family. Nowadays things have loosened but she knows his fierceness is only hidden beneath the surface and can erupt.

"You should never have bought that…"

"Who says?"

"I say."

"What's wrong with it – there's nowt wrong…"

"You should know better – have you no fucking sense – you stupid geek!"

"Don't you…"

Glasses breaking and then the thump of someone falling. A rabble of men's voices. Her heart banging.

Her mobile chirps. She rummages in her bag. Hamid's voice cuts her free of the past.

"Julie-Anne, you want me to come there?"

"No, Hamid, no, it's best I tell them on my own."

She pictures the Victorian house in a cul-de-sac by the park where Hamid lives. Rubbish bins overflow before the building. When the front door grates open, chill air hits your face. It must have been a handsome house in the 1890s but now it is a multi-occupancy place for doleys and people scraping by. In the hall, piles of circulars and mail for unknown people topple onto the floorboards and dither in the draught.

Hamid's room, three floors up, faces what must have been a garden now largely concreted over. A sycamore tree blazes shedding burnished leaves. He took her there first in the spring and it haunts her with its forlorn beauty. The vast room is dominated by the window rising from floor to ceiling. Patches of damp spread like ink blots on the wallpaper and the floor is covered by carpeting the texture of stringy brisket. The single electric fire gobbles coins. But even the cold can't diminish the thrill and strangeness of that room. It has secrets, like Hamid, that she will never know. In that room he held her for the first time and she trembled with the smell of his body and the shock of his closeness.

Now, sitting on her bed, she tries to plan how she will open the conversation but her attention veers about. It started in the college canteen with everyone pushing and shoving to the servery. Tubular metal table legs and chairs squeaked on floor tiles. Separated from her mates she found herself beside this man with the gunmetal complexion and bilberry coloured eyes.

"Are you student?" he said.

"Yes," she said not wanting a conversation. He must be an asylum

14

seeker and you didn't get involved with those. Girls who did were slags and such men didn't know how to treat women – they slapped them about and treated them like dirt.

"I am learning English."

"Oh."

Let him shut up. If only the queue would move down. Perhaps she could try to push in higher up but she didn't see anybody she knew.

"Are you local girl?"

"Yes."

"I am from Kurdistan."

"Right."

No chance of escape. They approached the counter.

"Can I sit with you?"

She tried to find an excuse but couldn't. "If you want."

He sat across from her and she didn't want to look at his glossy black hair and his darting eyes. She felt self-conscious. Anybody seeing her would think she was one of those girls who went with asylum seekers. Nobody else came near their table.

She battled with her lasagne and wished she'd bought a cheese and pickle sandwich and gone into the park to eat it.

"English is very difficult."

"I expect it is."

"When I first come here, I can't speak."

That was when she started to think of it: not being able to talk the language, not knowing anybody, escaping from somewhere. In the canteen at 12.30pm, she imagined the sheer horror of being unable to communicate, and it brought her out in a sweat. Cutlery rang on Formica tables and the talk and laughter all around clappered on her ears and skidded about. When she glanced up from her plate she met his eyes.

And saw they were sad.

On the way home that day she caught herself staring at people around her on the street – usually they were just the background to her life and she knew if she wanted to, or had to speak to someone, it would be quite easy. But what if it wasn't? What if all these people couldn't understand you, even hated you just because you came from somewhere else?

The next time in the canteen she looked for him but didn't see him. Perhaps she would never run into him again. Two days later leaving the college at 4.30pm, she turned and saw him crossing the concourse. Should she pretend she hadn't noticed him or should she go up to him?

"Hi," she called.

He caught her up. "Julie-Anne, how are you?" he said, putting the stress on the 'you'.

She said she was fine. As he walked beside her all the way to the bus station, she kept getting glances from other students and workers on their way home. They looked and then averted their eyes.

She knew now he used to work in his father's business; that his father and uncles were driven away in a truck never to return. He told her bits and the gaps suggested more than he managed to spell out. There were mountains and rough terrain, heat and winds to claw the skin off your face… music, men dancing in bright costumes… nomads.

"We are a persecuted people," he said.

All this was outside her experience. The words sounded in her head long after he had finished speaking.

"Mum and Dad," she will say, "I've been seeing someone for a long time – and I want to move in with him – and I am going to move in with him."

She can't say it – they will never accept Hamid. Everybody they know despises asylum seekers. They mess about with our girls and take our jobs; they're scroungers. They should all be sent back home, is her dad's view often stated, and what will the neighbours think?

This is how it will go… just as it did on the day Uncle Alan bought the dinghy from the Sea Bird, a trawler that sank with all hands on board. And Uncle Alan never did sail away into the blue out yonder as he'd planned. The boat disappeared and nobody would ever speak of it. Uncle Alan had been pulled into line so that nobody would complain.

She would die for Hamid but can she tell them? She must say it out. When Hamid touches her, the skin on her arms tingles – he is her dark prince. But she loves her fierce dad, knows he is proud of her.

If she doesn't break the news this evening, Hamid will think she has failed him, that she isn't serious. Why should she let the small-mindedness, the cruelty of other people affect her? Why not tell them and be done with it? She wants to vomit. The wind sighs against the house as she prepares to go downstairs…

THE BABY

Two days ago Jim watched, shoulders screwed up with tension, as an injured bat swooped to and fro, trapped in his local supermarket. It thundered into fixtures, shaved the strip-lighting and hit the plate-glass windows. His curiosity jumped and his imagination wove wild pictures, making him sweat in his navy suit. Jim felt that bat must be blundering about in his solar plexus.

Flat fields doze under a mottled sky. Outside the car windows, the road snakes by houses set amid prim, weed-free lawns and flowerbeds shrill with scarlet geraniums, white alyssum and deep blue lobelia. Nice regular people living in regular houses and who drink in the white-walled pubs festooned with a frenzy of hanging baskets.

Strange to think that the place should be hidden away in this peaceful landscape that suggests picnics and lazy afternoons, not walls closing in.

Claire can't understand why he has to do it. But what does it matter, she persists, – you loved your mum and dad – why must you start raking about?

He has asked himself this question many times. Claire has no dark corners in her life: all is transparent – she has two elderly parents, one crazy about golf; the other collecting antiques and playing bridge. He wouldn't be surprised if they can trace their pedigree back to William the Conqueror. She doesn't question who she is, doesn't need to excavate. He, on the other hand, has had two caring people – now dead – who were in no way related to him.

His own identity has remained a mystery, one which he has a compulsion to understand. His adoptive parents were a laid-back, easy-going couple with laughter-crumpled faces. They had blond hair and blue eyes. He on the other hand is black-haired, grey-eyed. Where they were squat and wide-boned, he is tall, loose-limbed, and given to swift mood swings. It is obvious that a particular conjunction of genes has created him. Details have unsettled him over the years.

On family photographs his difference from the rest of the family snags the eye. Official forms catch him in the same way. A probing question can unleash a sequence of introspection in him. One endless school holiday, when he was fourteen, a discussion on families with a mate forced him to ask, Mum, do you know anything about my natural parents? Instead of

17

treating his question in her easy everyday way, she'd looked shocked. They didn't tell you, she'd muttered. Who were 'they', he wondered but didn't like to press the matter, because a more definite answer might have killed his favourite fantasy of his father as a famous writer.

So the years passed until the morning when he was going through his mother's bureau after her death. She'd kept his early drawings and paintings and school reports, all neatly documented but beneath them he'd found the adoption certificate. His insides blundered about in his rib cage and he felt he was imprisoned behind plate glass, not knowing how to break free.

The sign leaps up without warning. He is almost there, but he can't meet this stranger without having worked out a strategy. Does he go, Hello, Dad? But how can he, when they don't know each other? Of course he could start with, Hello Norman. Even the name Norman sounds strange to him – but perhaps it was popular in its day. Mum and Dad might have felt hurt that he is doing this – they might consider it a repudiation of them, only it isn't like that. This is a journey he has to take because he must find the core of himself, know who he really is. Their dying has opened the way. Curiosity won't let him rest. He must find the truth.

Into his head come some words he jotted down in his Filofax:

Truth is too precious to tell every fool who asks for it

Perhaps he is a fool for wanting to know. Claire's complete incomprehension has made him feel that she for one considers he is wasting his time.

The huge complex squats on a plain; before it lies a car park; to the left, lawns and an estate of new brick houses. Jim parks, climbs out of his car, fastens his jacket and brushes sandwich crumbs from his trousers.

He approaches the front of the building, aware of the scrutiny of men in blue uniforms behind a bulletproof screen. They demand some form of ID and he produces his driving licence. He must remove his shoes, his watch, jacket; surrender his mobile phone; pass under a metal detector and be rubbed down. He feels vulnerable and at the same time outraged. Prison officers with clinking keys and radios marshal him towards an automatic door. This is it then.

Norman examines the leaves of the spider plant and spots a splodge of something sticky. He dabs a Jay-cloth at it and smoothes the long striped leaf with careful fingers. A microscopic creature scrabbles up the grape ivy and Norman pincers it between thumb and index finger, then stares at the brown splat and rushes to the sink to wash. He must get a move on with the dusting.

The floors have to be done before the classes come down. Such a rush today. Everything seems to be happening at once – so much dust and balls of paper, they will throw their tab ends about – such a lot of mess, always the rubbish.

Just when the staff room looked real nice with that tasselled cloth on and the roses – better than real because the petals won't fall off and make a mess – but – if only that Jane, bossy cow, wouldn't be such a tyrant: I don't like the flowers and the cloth I'm afraid, Norman – it's all cluttered. Plants on the bookshelf okay, but I'm afraid we can't have.

All that thought and the little homely touches gone to nothing. Always the same, always some bitch pushing and shoving – no you can't, Norman – you can't. Do this, Norman, do that!

Four tab ends under the table and six balls of paper, a broken biro and the wrapping paper off of a chocolate bar. Filthy creatures. No idea about personal cleanliness. May as well live in a sty some of 'em. A nice blast with the pine air-freshener.

Today is the day.

Norman has put a big red balloon round the date on his calendar since he got the letter. Every night for weeks lying in his pad, he has gazed at it. The whole thing makes him nervous, gives him pains in his stomach and a buzzing in his head. Buzz, buzz like some big fat bluebottle bombing against glass – buzz it goes. He wants to swat at it, but he can't because it's inside him, not out.

The cons come lumbering down from the wing, dragging their feet and dropping stuff here and there, making a racket. They barge into the classrooms. Some nod, "Hiya, Norm!" They try to wheedle round him, because they think he can nick tea bags, sugar, biros for them. After all, being an orderly, he gets access to areas they don't: they know he has certain information – stories he overhears. He's heard all sorts through gratings: words whispered, hints dropped.

See all, hear all, say nowt is the best policy. Just store it away, because you never know when it might come in handy.

Ten thirty. Coffee time. Tom – black, two sugars; Rachel – white no sugar; Brendan – tea, white one sugar; Jane – weed-killer and two sugars.

He taps on the classroom door. Rachel opens up and smiles at him. "Oh, thank you so much, that's great, Norman, just how I like it."

"Ooh apple for the teacher!" the cons holler. He takes no notice. Rachel is a nice lady, she's kind and tidy – everything's always lined up real straight on her desk.

This afternoon, August the fourteenth, the visit. The pains come again like so many blades. It isn't that he's forgotten the baby – no, he never has. The baby has always been there at the back of his mind. Now, this isn't just the baby, this is a man, a son, somebody called Jim Pollock. A peculiar name Pollock. Of course he had to have another name, him being adopted.

Perhaps this Jim Pollock has searched his mother out as well. Trixie was a girl with candyfloss hair and hearts in her ears, a pretty lass. He has this dream about him and Trixie and the baby all being together in the country, living in this cottage where there's a garden back and front and night scented stocks, phlox, hollyhocks and delphiniums grow by the front door because of the scent. At the back there'd be vegetables all in lines with runner beans climbing up canes and cabbages – everything neat and no weeds.

Just time to wash out the mugs; have a quick tidy round, then back to the wing for a wash and brush up. Beanie and Beakie twitter at him – he thinks he loves Beakie, the blue budgie, more than Beanie, the yellow.

He's been ready for three-quarters of an hour. His hands shake and he feels he might throw up. The buzzing drones on in his ears, deeper now, like a generator. It reminds him of just before they took him away in a white van. There he was in this street and he didn't know what to do; didn't know who he was or where he should go. He got acid churning his stomach and a lead taste in his mouth and the generator humming. People's eyes slid over him as though he was invisible and he knew that if he dropped dead out on the pavement, nobody would stop, they'd clatter on by.

Finally when the officers do come for him, he almost tells them, he's decided he doesn't want to see this man – but somehow he can't say it because he can't forget the baby and anyway he needs to know what's become of him, so he bumbles along with them to the visits room. On the way he stares at the corridors; the scabby bits on the plaster, a scuffed corner. He knows the clanging of the metal gates; boots on shiny flooring. They form patterns, patterns of his life. He doesn't want to get to the visits room. He has never had a visit before and he doesn't know what to do.

The afternoon burns. He watches it through the barred window. A working party, seen in the far distance through the scrolls of razor wire and the electrified metal fencing, look like matchstick men. Housemartins pirouette and swoop above the fence.

Then the man comes: the baby. Norman stares as he approaches but when the man sits down opposite him, he concentrates on scratching his arms.

"Hi," Jim says, shocked at the sight of this tall figure hunching at the table. The stranger appears curled in on himself and won't look up. His eyes stare at a point to the left of Jim's jacket pocket.

"Good to see you," Jim tries.

"Yes," the other man mutters. His voice is very soft. He seems far too mild, mild and lost. Jim expected someone more forceful.

"Have you been to see her?" the man asks.

"Who do you mean?"

"Trixie, your mother."

Why couldn't somebody have warned him that he'd have to break this news? He can't just pretend it's trivial. His shirt sticks to his back and his heart lurches as he struggles to find the words.

"Er right, well, I'm afraid this isn't going to be easy. Seems she died ten years ago."

Jim gets a shock as for the first time he meets the other man's eyes – his own eyes, grey striped. He sees the pain in his father's eyes, notices the tortoising of his father's head, a scaly head poking from a shell. Inside the shell is all the softness, the vulnerability, things he dare not know about.

"So Trixie's gone," his father says. "Never thought about that – she was such a young lass. She had to get you adopted, like – nothing she could do – was the mother – the mother."

"Yes," Jim says, sweating with clamminess and horror. He shouldn't have come to this place. He feels he is heaving up a stone slab and discovering all manner of obscene giant slugs beneath. The effort of raising the stone judders his heart. He doesn't want to see... He finds his own gaze has dropped away; he can't look at his father's face. His father is scratching himself and in so doing the sleeve of his T-shirt falls back and Jim sees his arm is scored with scars, like the rings on the bole of a tree; some are white lines, others raised red weals. He shudders but tries to conceal the involuntary movement.

"Aye, it was the mother – she stopped it. That was why I had to – of course they didn't understand. Trixie was a little cracker."

Jim doesn't know what to say. Why does his father want to make this confession now? He struggles with the idea that this other person, this

Trixie, the little cracker, has been his birth mother. 'Little cracker' suggests a sexual element and he doesn't want to know about that – this after all is somebody who gave birth to him. His dad seems to have run down now and a silence stretches between them.

"What's your job then, like?" The question shoots at him.

"Oh well – I'm a teacher."

"A teacher! You're a teacher!"

At the amazement and pleasure in his father's voice, Jim is able to look up and meet his eyes.

"And what is it that you teach?"

"English. You know, reading and writing."

"I like writing letters – write to one of them on Death Row in the States like. Used to be good at composition at school."

Time is up.

Jim rises and so does his father opposite him. The man holds out his hand and Jim takes it.

The man smiles.

"It's been a treat," he says, "a real treat to see you. I don't get no visits – first one in thirty years. I don't know no folk on the out now."

"No," Jim says stunned by the enormity of the sentence and what this implies. He stands awkwardly facing his father still trying to connect with his words. All his own lifetime his father has been shut away – weeks, months years of isolation. And he has spent those thirty years wrestling with his own cut-offness. He doesn't know what to say and his father seems equally uneasy and has started scratching his arms again. When his father finally breaks the silence, Jim finds himself gazing into his father's timid eyes.

"Don't suppose you'll want to come back again then, like?"

Jim can't help himself. "Oh yes, I'll be back, there's no doubt about that."

The officers clomp up and Norman tenses with the humiliation of being led away before his visitor. His son, a teacher! He wants to stay in the picture of that afternoon. He remembers the feel of the young man's hand. Over and over he returns to the long warm fingers, the way they grasped his, the hand holding – Trixie's baby. This fine young man is Trixie's baby and he'll come back for another visit

Back in his pad Beanie and Beakie twitter at him and Beanie beaks his thumbnail. He tells them about his son and then he sits fingering the scars on his arms and is glad he didn't cut any deeper.

JAMIE AND THE LADIES

Jamie follows the bristles as he pushes the brush down the landing, chasing tab ends and piles of dust and fluff. Somebody has slung a torn pair of boxers onto the safety net between the landings. For months the net will be clear and then one morning you'll see a half-eaten bread roll or a sock – even a plimsoll – lying there. Should he leap on and drag the boxers off? Better not. You can get a strike for climbing onto the safety net. At least cleaning stops you thinking all the time and dwelling on things. But they don't go away; they just stay there waiting for later.

Only two more weeks to go and he'll be out. And what then? Before he ever landed in here he cruised along nicely, no sweat. Loved up with Katie and what else did you need to think about; Katie with her long pale hair and the little chain with the heart on, dangling round her left ankle? Just her feet in the red dagger heels can set him going. She's this mixture of sophisticated woman and small kid. Everything about her is young and girlie, like her pink and white spotted underwear.

On the Twos he stops to admire a picture somebody's painted on the wall. He's often stared at it before because it brightens things up.

A prison officer sees him looking and stops. "That's where they used to top 'em," he says. "They'd jump down there and they fell through and the rope broke their necks."

"Oh, right," Jamie says and grins to fool the screw. He seems to have got a shudder stuck in his chest but he looks down at the pavers and keeps brushing. Better to think of Katie, that will make things all right. Of course nothing's easy. They were going to get married. He expected her to live with him in the caravan, but Katie had other ideas.

"That's what pikies do… I don't want to live in a caravan like them… it's dirty and it's cold."

He walked right into it, said they'll do whatever she wants. Only he's had other ideas since. Now he's not so sure. He has tried to live in a house, but with a house you can't just pack up after a couple of weeks and move somewhere else. You're pegged down. With a house you're a snail, you've got it on your back and you can't get rid; all the bills to pay and the roof to see to and the gas and the electric. You never finish. The minute you think you're sorted, something else is broke. No, a house makes everything a lot more complicated.

He keeps brushing. The lads are still banged up. They'll be let out soon. Must get the landings cleaned first. Once they're out you can't do much because they're in the way. They like to stand leaning on the rails bellowing down to guys on the Ones, or up to the Threes and Fours. Most of 'em spend their lives in here. They don't know any different and once they're out, they say they don't feel right – they think they will, and they tell one another stories about how great it's going to be, except that it isn't. Even in his time in there, he's already seen 'em coming back.

The fair will be moving on today – that's what he misses, the setting up; the feel of the new place. At night it'll all be going full throttle: rides thundering round and the music flaring; the lights winking; hot dogs frying, fat hissing and spitting; the lasses shrieking their throats off… Katie's had him living with her in this little brick house and he's had to leave her in bed and make for the fair. Folks thought he was a mad sod carrying on like that because he's not the type. He belongs to the fair, it's his. He can make money, always has had cash dribbling out of his pockets. It's like he can't lose. But he'd know she was still lying there, all soft and warm, and when he made it back, real late on, she'd be waiting for him between the white sheets.

The fellers getting their necks broke when they jumped through the trap makes him feel real jumpy. You'd never think that when you look at that picture of the countryside – the sun's shining and everything's bright green. You could imagine lying down in the grass. Katie's got these three brothers with sharp noses and rattish faces. You never know where you are with them.

"You'll see our Katie's all right of course, won't you?" the big one, Eddie said, and then this sly, real poky look came at him. He's had to jolly 'em along the best way he can, so the brother doesn't see it's made him uneasy.

He's never been a letter writer, can't spell, but since he's spent time in here, he's about written his hand off. It's like he can't stop.

First, daughter Milly writes,

> *Dear Dad*
> *You said you was going to send us some money but you never I can't manage with oliver by myself and getting him new shoes and everything*
> *Love you loads*
> *Milly*

Milly is eighteen and living on her own with a baby. She doesn't think he should be with Katie and she stirs things up between him and her mam, Elaine. Twenty years he's been married to Elaine.

"You don't know how to keep your trousers on," Elaine has told him. "It just does my head in."

"It's not my head it does in!" he's told her and he's laughed. She doesn't think it's funny and has left him.

Katie's letter arrives. Her writing is girly and the letters real chubby and she does little circles for dots. She uses pink paper and flowered envelopes with pink linings that smell scented.

> *Darling Jamie*
> *You said you was leaving us some cash only we haven't got it You never got them tattoos took off and you promised you would get that cow's tattoos off of your back and chest and you was going for a divorce but you never Things here aint easy we are just stuck I am not happy,*
> *Cheers Katie*

He spends all afternoon during bang-up writing to Katie and explaining that while he's in there, no way can he get the tattoos removed. He tries to be a bit lovey, calls her 'my own darling' and 'sweetie' and tells her he loves her to bits and can't wait to be with her and it will be all right and he thinks about her all the time and he'll make it up to her. He signs off 'all my love'.

The first time he met Katie, the fair had been at Scarborough. They'd just set up and the rides whizzed through the air; the big wheel swishing round with lasses screaming and clutching tight to the bars; on the golden horses some kids didn't want to come off, but there'd be the ones with big eyes hanging on like grim death. Fairs are great places for picking up lasses. They dawdle in, licking toffee apples and lollies, on the scout for excitement, and they want to be thrilled.

She was with her friend, Phoebe, a real scaredy-cat, but Katie was different right from the off. She wanted to go on all the rides, anything fast, and the sort that makes lasses scream. She was straight into the ghost train; got on the waltzers and you stood behind her and spun it until she yelled and screeched and her skirt blew up and you could see her flowered pants and her soft thighs.

She would have stayed there all night if she could have. Everyday they were pitched in Scarborough she turned up. Elaine always complained about him and how he couldn't get on with his job for sweet-talking lasses, and she noticed he let Katie go on the rides for free.

The Sunday morning they moved on, Katie came down early to say goodbye and she gave him her mobile number. Sometimes he wishes he never saw Katie sidling up with her lips round a lolly.

Soon he'll be finished brushing and then the lads will be unlocked for assoc until dinner. Will she write again? Waiting for the post makes his heart bang and that's crazy... why should he get excited about a letter? He never had letters before coming in here. Never wrote any, never received any... and now? If he doesn't get one, he worries. If they hand him one, he feels his heart bounding in his chest and he hardly dare open it, because he might not like what he sees. He spends a third of his wages on writing paper, envelopes and stamps. The screw thrusts two letters at him.

"Wilkinson, somebody loves you."

"Thank you, Mr. Johnson." He grins at the screw. Katie again. The other letter's from Elaine – but he'll leave that until later.

> *Dear Jamie*
> *You keep making all these excuses about why you never get them tattoos off and why you never get divorced but how do i know you wont do just the same when you get out? It's the same with the money.*
> *Cheers Katie*

He sits in his pad during bang-up and reads the letter again. Smithy in the top bunk has doled out his advice.

"Sack 'em off! If all they can think about while you're inside is cash, then sack 'em..." Smithy is a little bloke with a bull neck and colossal shoulders. He works out whenever they let him attend the gym.

Jamie finds his head flickering; nothing stays still but all sorts of moods zigzag to and fro. One minute he thinks he should do one thing, and the next the opposite. If she came on visits, he might be able to straighten things out, feel different but that's not the point – she's already started thinking stuff. He can make money, always has, never been a problem, but now with him being temporarily short, they're all whining.

He'll have to have a good think about this. When he first found himself in here, he freaked out... nobody knew, but looking back, he knows he did big time. But now there's two weeks to go and he gets to feel he'd be glad if it was two years instead.

Smithy is looking at him. "What's up mate?" he says, "You've no need to be down in the mouth now."

"It's not that easy," he says. He hasn't been thinking about Elaine lately. Katie badgering him all the time about not getting divorced has started to make him wonder why he hasn't bothered about it. Does he want a divorce or doesn't he? Elaine must be in it somewhere. She's got a weird hold on him. They have had the kids together, there is that, but what else? Elaine's not a bit like Katie… of course she's a lot older, but it isn't that. She's dark, goes in for drifty clothes, long skirts and shawls with fringes on, drop earrings and strings of beads and gold chains, but she understands horses and has three dogs and two cats.

When he thinks about it, he has to say she's a bit of a wild woman. He's put her through a lot and she's taken it, but Katie seems to have been the last straw. Perhaps the one he really loves is Elaine. It would get to him if he could never see Elaine again. Now he hasn't considered that before, because he's been concentrating so much on Katie and Katie's newness. Elaine wears leather boots with heavy soles and she strides out. Her face doesn't give much away.

He ought to read Elaine's letter now – he hasn't before, because he's getting tired of all these women demanding cash off of him. It's like that thing about kicking a dog when it's down. You bet your life, Elaine'll be bleating on about Katie and what about her cut. He rips the envelope open and stares at the jagged tears. Weird, he didn't know Elaine's hand-writing until he landed up in jail – married to her for 20 years and never seen it before. There's no flowered envelopes here; it's all plain white, no frills.

> *Dear Jamie*
> *Just writing to let you know I have taken charge of the fair. Me and Mally are going to run it from now on.*
> *All the best*
> *Elaine*

He's had a thump in his guts and he bellows with shock.

"Bad news?" Smithy says.

"Diabolical… she says she's taken over my fair… no way can she do that."

"Who's that then?"

"Elaine, the wife, I should have got a fucking divorce. She's screwing me well and proper, shafting me to hell… and who's this 'Mally'… 'Me and Mally', what's that about? 'Me and Mally'… so she's shacking up with him, that's her game…"

He wants to throw something, hurl everything in the pad out of the window, but he can't. Sweat trickles into his eyes. His fair, his life… she can't take it just like that… and this bastard, Mally, he'll get after him. Let him watch his back!

He sees her in her long skirt and her big boots and wearing his old coat as she strides round the rides and bosses everything. She was there when he stayed over in that red brick house with Katie. What was she doing then? How long has it all been steaming along between her and that Mally?

It should have been easy to sack her off… forget her… but it's not what he thought. He can't get free of her with her hawk's face and her dark eyes. But she left him, didn't she? Only she didn't really… she's been around ever since in her own caravan, always there. She's a fair woman born and bred. She's like him. They do things to each other, killing things that would finish most folks. Has she meant it this time? What if this is the end of the road between them?

"What'll you do about that then?" Smithy says.

"I could just do with a real long sentence," he says at last.

"You don't mean it!" Smithy says. "I've had some and it's not a bundle of laughs."

Jamie shudders, he can see the fair, all those wagons and caravans and the massive rides being lifted forward by powerful engines. Crows and gulls plunge down on the empty fairground to gorge on the leavings… But it's going without him! How can it, it's his fair? She can't do this to him…

THE DECISION

This shift can be either spooky but quiet or punctuated by alarms and weird incidents that put your teeth on edge.

Time for supper and Andy Mullet plugs the kettle in. He's bought a packet of cheese and pickle sandwiches from the canteen, and he can't wait to start eating. So far everything has been calm, though you never can bank on it. Night is the time when inmates start topping themselves or setting fire to their pads or tunnelling under the floor to have it away.

"Coffee's up!" he calls, and Wayne Shawcross barks, "Won't be a jiff." He must be washing his hands. Wayne washes his hands a lot; but then there's just something about this place that makes you feel you should be pushing your hands under the tap and scrubbing away at them with a germ-repellent wash – Aids, Hep' B and C and all kinds of other nasties might be wafting in the air and contaminate you. Andy won't dwell on them. Working in here, he has sometimes thought, is like being a scaffolder, or one of those guys who paint suspension bridges: you must get on with the job; once you start bellyaching about how far the drop is, you've caught the sickness, lost your nerve, and you'd better give up.

Wayne strides across to the table. "Made it, have you?"

"Aye... that's what I said."

"So you did."

They grin at each other.

"Not bad so far tonight," Andy chances.

"Don't say it," Wayne yawns, "I'm not in the mood for anything tonight."

"What's up then?"

"Oh, just tired," Wayne rubs his eyes. "It's working in here that tires me. Look how it's been today. First bit of sun we've had this summer. I could have done with getting out, but I have to go to bed, don't I..."

"Sure."

Andy doesn't listen, he's back in the afternoon watching Debbie undress – her day off and Brett, her husband, is on A shift, so she's free to lead her own life. He travels back into the surprise of her... Her little skirt drops to the floor, then she sheds her pure white blouse and stands before him. He moves across and fiddles with her bra fastening. Bewitched, he gazes at her firm apricot flesh and traces the golden down running from her belly-ring to her black lace thong. The tingling surges up from his ankles and seizes him in a wave of intense pleasure.

Wayne goes on talking. Andy doesn't want to come down off the crest. Oh, he's crazy for her... all those glimpses; the catching sight of her with Brett... after all, they are his neighbours, and Brett, being a colleague, meets him most days. Even during their off-duty they can't escape, because they'll be cheek by jowl in the mess next door to the canteen. At night he always fancies he hears their bed creaking. Only a thin wall separates one house from the next on this little purpose-built estate for prison officers and their families. The sound drives him into a fury of longing.

Since Gemma divorced him and took the kids, he has lived here alone, eating in the canteen and pushing down late-night snacks in front of telly, whilst working through six packs of lager. The pattern of changing shifts passes him at a distance; he is insulated from it by the thought of Debbie. His days are spent planning strategies for meeting her, or returning over their last time together. It's weird, he thinks, how everybody in here seems to be sex obsessed: the guys behind their doors because they aren't getting any; and his colleagues because they are... all those wives and girl friends just waiting for it.

They eat for a while in silence and then Wayne says, "I shall take Mandy and the kids away somewhere hot – going down to the travel agents next week. You get fed up with this lot in here."

"Yes," Andy says, "yes, you do."

The dogs set up a howling and both men listen. From the barred windows all you can see are electrified fences; coils of razor wire and arc lights drenching everywhere in a hard white beam. Everything is under surveillance. Police cars circle the perimeter twenty-four hours a day, purring forward in a sleek unobtrusive way like killer sharks.

"Do you know, when I first came to work here, I was dead curious to know what they'd all done... now I don't want to hear anymore... can't be doing with it." Wayne chomps down his sandwich and frowns.

"Going to the match next Saturday?" Andy asks.

"No chance. If I'm off, then it's decorating... got to take Mandy into town to get some paint and wallpaper."

"Sooner you..."

"Yer, yer. At home you spend life working and then you get here and there's Blakey trying to top hisself and you think, get on with it, mate. Moore complaining that his mail's been tampered with; Wallace gets stabbed by that con two pads up... I mean, there's no end to it. Shoot 'em all, that's what I say."

"We'd be out of a job if they did!" Andy laughs.

"I'd say thank Christ."

"It's a wage, man, and there's your pension."

"Aye, in thirty years time… don't tell me."

Wayne pauses, then starts again, "Kids get you down."

"How do you mean?"

"Well, there's our Shona… thirteen going on twenty-three; wants to go clubbing. I mean, you don't know what to do with 'em. I said to Mandy, she's not going, she's only a kid. I mean, anything can happen to young lasses these days. Think of all this lot in here and what they done. If you add up all the lasses they've raped and murdered…"

The dogs' howling drifts across the night. Somewhere a voice screeches; something heavy crashes. Owls moo.

Andy goes to stand at the barred window and stares out over the prison compound. The stalag enclosures rise up like so many Chinese boxes, glinting in the arc lights and the moon floats clear of a cloud mass; the paths shine bone-white. A great dark bird flaps by; the dogs yowl. Nothing stirs. He can see lights from the special unit away at the far end of the compound.

It's been a strange pellucid day with amber light and heat tempting out late bees and dozy wasps and ochre and bronze leaves drifting down from the trees, but with the coming of evening a dankness has seeped up and now a winter chill has fallen.

"I don't like working in this unit," Wayne says, "sooner be with ordinary cons – thieves and the like, not these." He opens a second packet of sandwiches. "Want one?"

"What are they?"

"Ham."

"Go on then, ta."

A buzzer pings and a light shows on the console. Somebody thumps on a pad door.

"Let the tosser wait!" Wayne concentrates on his sandwich, "Do you know, I wouldn't mind a brew of tea now – coffee doesn't slake your thirst the same."

"Okay, I'll fill up again." Andy goes off to the tap. The light blimps. He can still hear the pinging.

"They think they can just snap their fingers and we'll come running… like kids that's what they are, and bulk of 'em shouldn't be in a nick.

They're mental… should be in a nut house." Wayne continues to chew, his face screwed up with annoyance.

"It's Trent in 14," Andy says, looking at the console.

"I know. He's doing fourty-five years… every time he's got out, he's done a kid. He'll not be getting out any more though."

Andy pictures Trent, a skinny, athletic chap, always either in the gym or the chapel and given to painting crucifixion pictures and writing rhyming poems to his dead mother and Princess Di. From the look of him, you'd never guess his crimes, or perhaps you would… there's something in his very blue eyes, a mad staring quality. It's always the eyes that tell you. 'The eyes are windows of the soul,' he once read.

"Pour us a mug, and, don't know what it is about in here but it dehydrates you… maybe it's the ventilation system." Wayne chunters on. The light beacons on the console and the bell continues to shrill. "They say you can get a load of diseases from air-conditioning systems… well, I mean, they encourage bugs to thrive, don't they. What's that thing all those pensioners died of – legionnaires what's-it? That was air-conditioning caused it."

"Oh."

The light flickers and the buzzer drones as though it will never stop. The hammering on the pad door is desperate now.

Andy pretends he can't hear. He pours himself a mug of tea too and stirs in two sugars.

"We spend our lives making sure that the cons on the other unit never get at these wankers, and sometimes I think we should let 'em loose on 'em…" Wayne says.

Andy nods. "Too right."

Then as he sits at the table with the mug of tea steaming before him, Andy thinks, heart attack. The two words stick pins in him. Unconnected fragments jangle in his head. A couple of months back his dad was found dead, alone in his house. Heart attack, they said. Andy was telephoned at work by his dad's neighbour. Of course he attended the funeral but he hasn't thought about it much since, because he has been in the dream, of Debbie. Now with the words 'heart attack' ringing in his head, he comes alert. The ringing is Trent's bell.

Andy sees his dad quite alone in the sitting room with the pictures of Andy and his sister, Carole, in silver frames on the mantelpiece, staring down, as he struggles with the vicelike contractions of his heart. He cries out but nobody hears him. There's nobody to save him… nobody to call an ambulance. Sweat blisters his face.

Another picture superimposes itself on that one: Trent's face appears and becomes so vivid that it is almost as though Andy can see into his cell. The middle-aged figure clutches his chest. Sweat stands out in bright globules on his forehead. He presses the alarm buzzer, and falls to his knees.

"We'd better go to Trent," Andy says, looking across at Wayne.

"What for?"

"He might be having a heart attack."

"So bloody what? Let him have one… what use is he to man or beast… good riddance, I'd say."

"I'll go."

"Don't be daft. How would you feel if it was your bairn he done?"

"We're not here to judge." Andy can see Wayne doesn't like him arguing.

"Come off it… he'll stop ringing when he's had enough."

"You go on patrol. I'm going to his pad."

Wayne gives him a strange look. "Don't turn into a do-gooder, kid, because if you do, this job'll break you… there aren't any returns."

Andy doesn't answer but sets off down the long labyrinthine corridor, listening to the sharp sounds his boots cut in the asthmatic silence. He is driven by a sense of urgency, praying that he'll be in time…

THE PIGEON

On the day the judge pronounced sentence, Mark Smith's skin froze. Twenty years before any chance of parole! He was thirty, but by the time he was free he'd be old. How could you take that in – it was too large a chunk of a life. Perhaps he never would get on the out again – in twenty years he might be dead, dead in prison. It did happen. Better stop thinking about it or he'd go off his head. And what about Lisa? She'd never wait that long… anyway you couldn't expect it – she was twenty-four and she'd want sex, kids… with a face and body like hers she was bound to be mobbed. Just imagining what she was doing when he wasn't there could drive him crazy.

When cons got a long sentence they were often put on suicide watch in the hospital – but he hadn't wanted that. Being down there with all sorts of no-hopers and guys with HIV, self harmers slicing their ears off and worse, was not for him. Better keep it all buttoned up. He hadn't kicked off at the trial or when he got sent down for the twenty-year stretch. The papers said he gave no sign of remorse.

Since then he'd had plenty of time to mull over things. Did he feel remorse, no, not a bit, only anger. All right the guy was dead. The judge said he'd killed him. Not that he'd been on his own – Mick, Al, Boothy and Jenks had all joined in… though he'd got the longest sentence. He was supposed, according to the judge, to be the ringleader. The mug shots of them in the papers made them look a scary lot. When he'd seen this dumb, brutish face staring out at him, he'd been annoyed. It was nothing like him. Everyone said he was handsome – and anyway he had a lot of pull with lasses.

He'd written to Lisa after the sentence enclosing a V.O.

> *Dear Lisa,*
> *ta for coming to court. i was real choked to see you there. keep thinking about you all the time. Not much happens here. Exercise is at 8 am and if you're not ready, you don't get out except for half an hour later on. food is crap Got a job cleaning on the wing.*
> *Can't wait to see you.*
> *love you loads*
> *Mark*

She came in a micro-mini and stilettos. Her top plunged in a deep V and as she sat opposite him, he could gaze down it and imagine. She held his hand across the table. He wanted to tell her how his insides were caught in a vice that pressed tighter and tighter, but he couldn't. Just sitting with her, feeling the softness of her hands and having her scent in his nostrils made him nervous and his head ached, anger and irritation flickered near the surface but he mustn't let her realise... This couldn't last – who would she be seeing when she left the nick? He noticed the way the other cons and the screws ran their eyes over her... he wanted to beat them all to pulp. Stamp on 'em until there was just meat. Before all this... before it happened, he'd been in love with her... yes, of course he had, but somehow there hadn't been such an edge to it. He hadn't looked at her in the same way. Now she filled him with yearning because he couldn't have her like before. She'd be packed full of secrets.

When she'd gone, he sank into gloom. He had to admit to himself, he hadn't really enjoyed the visit, it was too fraught with stuff you couldn't say. One day she'd come and she'd just drop out that it was over... or she'd send a dear john to tell him. He'd meant to ask her if she wanted to break off with him, but when it came to it, he couldn't.

He didn't talk much to his pad mate but spent most of his time thinking about his case and wondering whether he should launch an appeal against his sentence – perhaps they hadn't killed the guy after all – somebody else could have later. He didn't think his lawyer had been good enough; he ought to have sacked him. His pad mate managed to filch him some file paper from Education and he spent the hours banged up in his pad trying to write down how the man got killed – this was not something he found easy to recall. It had got smudged like a picture that somebody had rubbed their arm over when the paint was still wet. He'd always been rubbish at English and even just writing letters put him in a sweat.

Late at night you'd been out clubbing with the lads before being ejected by this geeky doorman for mouthing off... but obviously you wouldn't mention anything like that. Feeling really peeved, you'd invaded another watering hole, the late-nighter that stayed open until 4 am. By this time you were well pilled up. You decided on a takeaway – you could generally find some kebab place or a burger joint still serving. On this night though, they were all shut. You were starving; the buzz had begun to wear off and Boothy and Al were being really annoying. It was then you saw the tramp. He was disgusting, filthy and he stank, was sleeping rough – quite honestly an eyesore... shouldn't be allowed. They're usually violent as well... he was a wino. You are not a violent person. This had nothing to do with violence, not really.

Boothy was the first to kick him. The tramp was curled up in a doorway near the kebab place. When he felt Boothy's shoe, the fellow reared up and shouted, brandishing a stick. That's when it all fired up. The wino was revolting. You got into kicking him – you heard the thud of your shoes against him and it was a bit like kicking a ball only instead of it being rubbery but resistant, this gave and was more like putting your feet into a bundle of rags. The wino let out a screech, a revolting tearing sound. Blood came spurting out of his mouth and trickled down his chin.

A car drove up at this point and slowed down. You told the others to pack it in, you left the wino and legged it. You didn't think he was dead – no, just beaten up a bit... but then he deserved it, didn't he... being like that. No decent person should be in that condition. It wasn't really violence... it was just something that happened... an accident. If the wino hadn't been there then; if they hadn't been hungry; if the kebab joint had been open... You wonder whether some of these merchants really want to run a business or not.

The car driver must have spragged on them and the next thing the Old Bill were on the track. You still couldn't get over the fact of getting twenty years for a geeky wino.

The writing had now become his case – he was working on his case. Well, most of the guys scribbled away on their cases. It was what you mentioned on the wing as a matter of course. Or you got a solicitor turning up with a smart executive case – but that cost and anyway, you'd still have to say what happened... but he'd get a solicitor in the end. All the time you heard about these miscarriages of justice.

Association. He wandered out onto the wing where a group played pool. Guys were on the phone home and queues had formed and those waiting for their turn pulled faces and heckled – everybody wanted to phone. Before you knew what, it would be bang-up and you'd have no chance until next day. The growing hubbub round the phones stopped. A pigeon had swooped low over the wing and then strafed the safety net between the landings as it tried to find its way out.

"Look there!" someone yelled. They centred on the bird. It was an event. Nothing ever happened on the wing so this was a bonus.

At first he didn't pay much attention but remained on the Twos staring vaguely before him and then the commotion below drew him in. Those on the Ones had started hurling the cones at the bird, the ones that the cleaners used to warn people to keep off damp floors. The cones flew up and clattered down. The bird flapped in frantic zigzags.

The cons bellowed, "Ger him, quick!" Their faces were screwed up with glee and the determination to fetch the bird down.

He glimpsed its breast feathers vibrating with the frenzied pumping of its heart. The bird was innocent… why did they want to kill an innocent creature? What was it in them that had transformed them in a fraction of a second into rabid dogs? Bile surged up his chest, was bitter in his mouth and he wanted to vomit. He couldn't bear to see how this would end.

Heart pounding he leapt down the stairs to the Ones. "Pack it in guys," he bellowed, "what's the point?"

A few looked round amazed, others took no notice, but then the screw came.

"Time for bang up," he said.

"What about that pigeon," someone said.

"Leave it." The screw couldn't be bothered. He just wanted to get them locked up for the night.

Mark shot through into the showers and made sure the air vent high up in the wall was open and wedged the shower door back with a cleaning cone. The screw didn't notice. He was pulling cell doors shut.

That night he didn't write anymore and his pad mate looking across at him said, "Not doing any writing then?"

"Na…"

He was in the grip of a fever and lay awake a long time and when he finally slept, he saw the pigeon banging crazily to and fro, its eyes staring out of its narrow skull, and then the pigeon changed into a man with stringy unwashed hair and broken teeth, blood seeping from his nose and mouth. Panicky and sweating he jerked awake.

SCENTS

My nose pulls me to the perfume counter and the line of testers. Which one first? The two assistants have their backs to me and natter together, so I don't have to worry about them.

I press the tester nozzle and a fine spray hits my wrist. I close my eyes and breathe the deep, spicy scent of sandalwood. I'm fifteen again and in my home town. I'm out with Janice, twagging from school and in the Quay, standing on the second floor, staring down at people wandering about: mothers with buggies, old folk, weird blokes who peer at young lasses. There are some kids from our estate twagging as well. I can smell the scent of the Indian shop on my skin – scarves, strings of beads, bracelets, incense. They make you think of elephants and brown skinned people with velvety pansy eyes, wafty saris, feet in gold sandals and tinkling anklets.

That's when I see Ben, the big one with the blue-black hair, riding the down escalator. He has spotted us and I know he'll come up.

The assistants are still in the middle of a story and so I spray on a Dior number this time. It isn't sweet with no centre – not one of those sickly, light smells. This is rich and expensive like diamonds and stilettos with four inch dagger heels – fizzy shoes in soft suede, the kind you hold in your hands to sniff the leather; or heavy, damson-coloured velvet curtains. That scent is about money; people sliding their legs into low-slung, gunmetal cars or black ones with a mica sparkle.

The blond assistant looks as though she's been on a sun-bed or living in the West Indies. Her scarlet lips smile. She's finished her conversation and asks me if she can help. I don't know what to say, but I mutter about just looking. I want to rush off then, but can't, because I don't want to stop spraying myself.

The testers squirt mist on my skin and I bend my head to breathe it in. The scent tingles in my nose and sets off vibrations all over me.

The thing about perfume is it can make you deaf and blind to everything else; it enslaves you, mesmerizes you. It's like immersing yourself in a deep, warm, bubble bath… only better. It transforms everything around you.

I spray something with a French name. It smells aloof, not sweet and not hot, but kind of cool, smart and sophisticated.

The assistant keeps looking at me, but pretending she's not. She studies her silver nails and I know she has her antennae out and she's thinking, only young girls go mad with perfume testers, so what am I – a grown woman – doing?

The next one is musky and hot – it reminds me of Ben's body spray. I can see his tar-black hair and the creases on his forehead when he explained stuff; the way he walked with a swagger from the hips, and you couldn't stop gazing at the tightness of his bum.

I daren't spray anymore with the assistant just waiting for me to push off.

All these different smells are in my nose and I keep sniffing at my wrists. I don't know how long I've been in the store. These people make me nervous. My insides growl and bubble and I feel a bit sick. Everything comes at me and I just want to escape.

As I move towards the doors, they slide open automatically and I'm in the street again.

Your nose gets used to scents so you can't smell them any longer. That's how I got with Mam's duty frees. She'd roll up with Boss, Chanel, CK, and I tried them all until she pounced, "You've been at my scent again!"

Ben once gave me a spray in a red bottle with jimpy sides and I sprayed it on my neck, down my thong and on my wrists. But I didn't know he'd nicked it.

I walk away from Boots smelling the perfume that drifts about me in a magic cloud. I can still see Ben how he was. He'd got the sort of body that made you want to look - not bulgy, pumped up muscles, just sculpted like a stone statue, the sort you see in parks, or the white marble ones in country houses and museums. I couldn't stop gazing at him and it made me feel weak, as though I wasn't myself any more, because I couldn't resist him. But girls loved Ben and he shared himself about.

Oh, it doesn't mean anything, he said, not important... I only really love you... Only to me, it did matter – I didn't want to share him... why did he need somebody else? Whenever I thought of him with them, with my best mate, Janice, it made my heart bang and I'd go all hot and crazy and feel I couldn't bear it.

In the street, cars whiz past and the air smells of exhaust. Tourists are taking photographs. The crowd presses in. My T-shirt feels damp. I can't seem to keep breath in my lungs. My hands shake. I raise my right wrist to my nose and I breathe deeply. All the scents are mixed up now. It seems very strange to be in this city that I don't know, though I've lived here for years and never been part of it. I don't belong here. Everybody is on the phone or texting. They're talking away to invisible people; crowds upon crowds of families, lovers, business contacts, all somewhere else. Hardly anybody is silent. Only me.

It felt better in the store. Outside is shifting all the time and it spreads out wide and makes me anxious. Anything could happen. I've got this scared feeling in my gut, the sort you get when you know something awful could happen. And I've no idea why I'm so frightened. If I could work that out, maybe it wouldn't be so bad and I could stop panicking. What if I drop down in a faint? Go mad? Behave in a weird way that'll make people notice me? I don't want anybody staring at me. What if they realize who I am? I look different now, I'm a lot older – the papers don't know what I'm like now. Miss Williams said she'd be sitting on the line of seats and she is. As soon as I spot her, I calm down.

"Did you like it in there, Tina?" she says.

"Yes, it was all right."

"Did you get what you wanted?"

"No," I say, "I didn't bother." Truth is, I've forgotten what I said I'd buy. Perhaps next time...

"What about an ice? You said you fancied one."

"Great!" I've dreamed of having an ice in a tall frosted glass with cherries and peaches and whipped cream on the top standing in peaks and with a chocolate stick stuck in it. I've often tried to remember that taste, but it's harder to recall than songs or even a smell.

I follow her into this café. Women gossip at little tables and there's couples whispering at each other and not seeing anybody else. It makes me nervous but I tell myself I'm all right.

"Are you enjoying it then?" Miss Williams asks again as though she's seeking reassurance.

"Yes, it's good," I say – but I don't know whether I'm enjoying it or not, because I don't feel comfortable; all the time I've got this bubbling in my stomach.

There's a short wait and then the ice arrives. Miss Williams is having a cappuccino and an iced bun. I pick out the chocolate stick and bite a piece off, and the sweetness floods my mouth. The cream blends with the dark brown taste and it's cool on my tongue. I delve into the glass and discover strawberries. It's like when I sprayed the perfume, and I close my eyes. Oh... I'd forgotten it could be so perfect. I don't ever want it to finish and I make it last a long time. Miss Williams has eaten her iced bun and is waiting.

"You won't have had one of those for a long time," she says.

"No," I say, "It'll be about fourteen years since I did."

"All set," she says, when I've licked the spoon dry and laid it down with a sigh.

"Yes," I say, "I'm all ready now."

A taxi pulls up then and we get in. When we arrive in front of the big brick fortress, we have to wait for a few minutes and then the automatic gates swing open and we drive into the forecourt. What a relief to be back! I'm safe now. I feel I've got too much to think about, and it will take me ages to digest the day.

COUNTING STARS

It was that annoying sort of night, when the punters wouldn't drink up and go home. The sound system had died out with a hiccup and the resulting silence usually jerked them into an awareness that the evening was over. But not this time.

"Come on mate," Steve coaxed, "time to go." The man he was trying to ease out had a shaven head, reptilian eyes and a nose like a wood pigeon's beak.

He stared back at Steve. "What you on about? I'm still drinking."

"Sorry, mate, but we're trying to close up. Everybody's leaving. You don't want to spend the night locked in here now, do you?"

The man's answer was a scowl. This was where you ended up having to manhandle them, because cajoling didn't work... Edgy stuff. You couldn't afford to hurt somebody and lose your badge. This was the last job on earth he wanted to do. It had been a standby years ago, but when you'd got to know the world a bit, you didn't need the hassle. These very late nights meant you couldn't keep tabs on what was happening at home. All night he'd not been able to focus his attention on the job. What a weird day... must have been 2.30pm when the phone had rung.

"...Mr. Slater – this is Janet Wilson, Headmistress at the The High School. I'm just checking that your daughter is at home with you."

"At home?" That had been a shock. "She went to school this morning and I naturally thought she'd be there with you now..."

That set Miss Wilson into a dither. It had upset him too. If Vicky wasn't at school, where the hell was she? He'd texted Lindsey at work immediately after he put the phone down.

He was in the middle of washing the kitchen floor and the mop stood in a bucket of muddy water. The strip near the door shone pink where he'd scrubbed mud and smears away. With news like this, you didn't want to carry on cleaning. First reaction: start phoning round the mates' houses... but they'd be at school. Perhaps better go out on the bike searching... but where?

A muddy, humid November afternoon, too warm for this time of year. 'Un-seasonal' people kept saying. Where the hell could she have got to? If she hadn't gone to school, where was she? There were all these stories of young girls seized by passing men in cars and vans who'd followed them, and dragged them in. Then you'd see pictures of the girls on telly and hear the distraught parents appealing for news, desperate to find their daughters. As the days passed the appeals grew more pathetic, and the mothers would come on, voices breaking … Eventually some dog-walker would discover a body…

At this point he felt quite sick. He had to do something but he couldn't leave the mess in the kitchen. He'd attacked the floor again, scrubbing and mopping until the sweat trickled down his forehead. A plan of action formed in his head: he'd start phoning her friends as soon as school finished. Most should be at home by 4pm. After that he'd be ringing the police. They'd have to do something. Once he'd got the plan, he didn't feel so bad.

Lindsey had texted back wanting to know if he'd discovered Vicky's whereabouts. He didn't want to have to go over it all again. The more he thought about Vicky's disappearance, the worse he jittered. He watched the clock, edging it toward 4, so that he could start phoning. Lindsey wouldn't be home until about 5.30pm to 6.

Dead on 4 o'clock the garden gate clicked. Steve stopped frying the chopped onion and minced beef for the chilli con carne, drew the pan off the heat, and looked round. Vicky sauntered in and slung her school bag on the sofa with an air of studied weariness. Steve turned to face her.

"Hiya, Dad," she muttered. "Just going to get my homework done." She'd been about to make off upstairs to her room – the last thing she would normally have done. Homework was a bad word and she generally had to be bullied into it. On arrival at home she'd be searching for the chocolate bickies or she'd toast a couple of slices of bread and make a jam sandwich, leaving toast speckles all over the table and gobs of jam. Later he'd find jam in the marg.

"Hold on, Vicky," he said. "Don't go wandering off, I want a word." He could see the guilt on her face. She tried to smile and make everything seem matey, pulling the 'little girl charm'. He wasn't having any. A wave of fury made his chest burn. All afternoon there he'd been worried out of his mind … he could just imagine Lindsey going spare as well.

"Where were you?" he said. He watched the colour flood her cheeks.

"How do you mean?"

She was trying to look surprised, and that annoyed him even more.

"You tell me."

She looked uncomfortable, not sure what to say. He didn't intend to let her slide out of this one.

"I don't understand, Dad."

"I think you do."

Her face was bright pink now, and he wondered how long she could continue with this farce.

"I'm not sure what you're on about…"

"Yes you are. You never went to school today, did you?" She dropped all pretence of humouring him and stood in front of him, staring at the carpet.

"If there's one thing I can't stand, it's lying, Vicky. That's what annoys me more than anything else. You've lied through your teeth – you must think I'm weak in the head not to spot it. So where have you been?" Her eyes filled with tears. That infuriated him even more – all ploys to gain sympathy and deflect his rage. He wouldn't let her off the hook.

"So where were you then?"

Silence. Her eyes still focused on the carpet.

"I suppose you're thinking up another lie – is that it?"

"No, Dad, I'm not…"

"Well then, where were you?"

"With some friends."

"Friends! What friends?"

"Nick."

"Who's Nick?"

"Someone I know."

A shout came from nowhere and his head pounded. "Who?"

"He's a boy I got to know at a party."

"And why wasn't he at school?"

"He's finished school."

"Yes, I'm sure he has … and he'll have no job and no likelihood of getting one." He blazed away, anger throbbing in his chest. This was how it went: she'd throw away all her chances, fail at school, find herself in a hopeless job – if she could ever get one.

"Can't you see what you're doing?" he bellowed. "You've missed lessons – soon you'll have mocks and you'll not be ready. Can't you see that if you hang about with some bone-headed kid and don't put your back into it and work, you'll end up with nothing, a loser?"

Fat tears bowled down her cheeks.

"So where did you see this Nick?"

"At his mum's – she was at work."

"Yes, I'm sure she was… working to keep her layabout son."

"Dad, he's not like that."

"Don't tell me… I don't want to know. Just get out of my sight!"

She seized her school bag and disappeared upstairs.

He'd carried on cooking the chilli and put a pan of rice on to boil. The stupid child… kids of her age went crazy, couldn't concentrate at school. What would become of her? She'd end up living with some lad, have a couple of kids, he'd clear off and she'd wonder what to do… no cash, no job, no qualifications, on her own with her two kids to bring up. It happened all the time.

"Come on, mate, got to go."

What a bloody mad-making day – aggravating punters like that merchant… and Vicky… She'd not come down for her tea. He'd not wanted to see her anyway. "Let her stew in her own juice," he'd said to Lindsey.

"Sorry, mate, can't wait any longer – you've been told."

"Oh, it's like that, is it!" Now the punter was on his feet and squaring up. He made a lunge at Steve and bumped against the table. The glass crashed to the floor spraying beer everywhere.

Steve got him in an arm lock, didn't speak, just marched him to the door, where his fellow bouncers were waiting to shoot the bolts and lock up for the night.

Ejected from the club, the man swore and shambled off vowing vengeance. The colleagues effed and blinded about the drunken chap and then settled down into a general grouse over the annoying nature of the customers and the way even when you felt like swatting them, you mustn't or you'd be caught on the CCTV and that could mean loss of badge, work etc. Everybody was scrabbling for the rapidly decreasing number of jobs.

Steve didn't say much; he restricted himself to joining in now and then with mumbles like, 'You're dead right there' and 'Too right…'

At last he could set off for home on his motor bike. The earlier damp fogginess had cleared and the sky was a glossy indigo, sprinkled with stars. What a relief to be in the open air, away from the claustrophobia of the night club. He liked returning in the early hours, because he met very little traffic and all the streets lay still, as though under a magic spell. You heard no sound; even the gulls must have gone to roost and the trains had stopped moving.

Lindsey had gone to bed hours ago and Steve moved about the kitchen in his sock-feet, making himself a mug of tea.

What about Vicky? He'd not seen her again before he'd left for work. The afternoon scene still lay between them. For sure he'd shocked her by his rage. But she'd lied... how much more twagging off would she have done, had she not been caught this time. Her dishonesty rankled – that wasn't something you could write off easily.

After rinsing out his mug, he padded up stairs, and decided to fetch Vicky. He found her asleep and wondered fleetingly if he should wake her – but hell, it was Saturday!

"Vicky!" he said. Her eyelids flickered open and she jerked upright, fear on her face. "Come downstairs for a minute, I want to show you something and have a talk."

The girl, shrouded in her dressing gown followed him into the kitchen. He unbolted the back door and motioned her to come out with him. They stood side by side on the doorstep.

"Look, Vicky, I'm sorry for going off on one earlier, but don't do any more lying. In the end people get so they don't believe anything you say any more – and that's sad. Your word is all you've got, you know."

She stood staring out and didn't speak.

"See those stars up there, they're wondrous, aren't they? I wanted you to see them. They'll be around until the end of time. They're bigger than we are, greater than all our little troubles. Aim for the stars. Think about those when you're tempted to do something daft, and they'll stop you."

"Sorry, Dad," she said.

He smiled at her. "Come on love, let's get in, and I'll put a pot of tea on."

CHARLIE

They used to say to her, "Dot, you're as tough as old boots!" She just smiled and carried on gutting. In the old days the place throbbed with life: galvanised crates grated together, bobbers' clogs clattered, gulls caterwauled and the stink of fish clogged your nostrils until you could no longer smell it. Dot were a fish-house lass and when she sat on the fish-dock bus going home, she reeked of it.

Dot flopped like a plastic bag crammed with groceries into her stripy deckchair in the yard. She can recreate that time when she heard the mooing of ships' hooters out on the Humber, and watched the men in their rubber boots lugging crates on the quay. Sun glinted on fish scales and those dead eyes. Fish were beautiful, so sleek and whippy, and she loved the herring's dark stripes and the marigold spots of the plaice.

These days Dot lives increasingly in her head – what else can you do when you can't get out because your knees have gone?

Sometimes the Charlie nights sneak back: Charlie, the love of her life, in his Waistell suit and with his jetty hair brylcreemed flat to his skull. Fresh off his trawler he called for her. His hawser arms twined round her waist. His chest, hard enough to terrify, was all muscle, honed hauling nets out on the North Sea. A body like his could crush you to death. He'd tell her about the white hell out in Greenland. That's how it was, he said, when the Ross Cleveland went down.

But in Rayner's pub he'd be at the bar buying the drinks in, pints and shorts for himself, and sweet sherry for her. The glamour was on him then as he ordered, and she watched the play of his shoulders and the light on his shiny hair.

Charlie was after her from the start. Fifteen and never been out with a boy, she spotted him on Dock Street off to the docks and he winked at her. "I'll take you out when I come back," he said. Not, Can I? Do you want to...? No, just I will.

She dreamed about him for the next fortnight, and shivered and her belly ached and fluttered.

When he rapped their front door knocker, her Nana said, "What does he want? You'll not go with him, he's on trawlers – anyway, you're too young." Nana turned him away with a flea in his ear. "His mam's got that many kiddies she doesn't know what to do. And they drink."

DAPHNE GLAZER

‖‖‖

She was twenty-one when he married her and twenty-one and a quarter when his trawler sank with all hands.

He shocked her, bedazzled her, and in a blink he was gone. Her wedding photograph in the silver-plated frame, a present from her niece, Sue, stands on the mantelpiece staring out. She's the smiling virgin bride, and he has a brooding, saturnine look. Now he seems so young to her, a grandson could have been his age, but on the day of that picture he'd been older than her, his face sly with experience.

Sue always tells her, "Aunty, you should move. This is not a nice neighbourhood, and one of these days you'll get broken into."

"It's what I know, lass, and I don't want to move – I'm all right here."

"You'd be fine in sheltered housing."

"What do I want with sheltered whatsit! I'm grand as I am."

In the yard with the July sun on her knees and a bit of breeze to cool it down, she can't imagine why Sue keeps on about it being a dangerous area and how she knows Aunty Dots must be having a struggle… All right, yes, when she has to rise from the deckchair, it will be a battle. Might take quite a while, and it does. She tries to drag her backside to the edge of the wooden frame. The deckchair tilts. She must force her knees to take the weight as she totters upright, lurches and almost falls.

When Charlie went, and she didn't want to see anybody and couldn't be bothered to be civil, his brother, Frank, paid court. Then along came his best friend Art, and later, Bri, a trawler man from down the street. They reckoned she'd want to forget her widowhood, but she didn't and never has. They thought she'd come round after a while, but now they know she won't, and it's a situation they can't understand, so they've told her she's hard as nails, tough as old boots. When she could still walk to the shops, she'd run into Bri, bowed now and leaning on a stick. He was full of his triple bypass operation and she had to shout because he was deaf and couldn't manage his hearing aid that buzzed like a demented wasp and drowned out conversation.

One day Bri asked her, "Why did you never fancy us then?" The words came at her, fizzing from the hearing aid.

"Well, Bri," she told him, going carefully, "You weren't Charlie… there's only ever been Charlie for me. Don't get me wrong though, I've always loved trawler men – what arms they had on 'em!" And she gave him her best smile that hinted at things, and would still keep him wondering.

They're talking about pulling this house down. For one thing there's no inside toilet, but she's used to that. It makes Sue shudder.

"Aunty Dots, you don't want to be living in a place like this and it's all full of holes. Thieves could be in here easy peasy."

She doesn't think about robbers, at least not until lying in bed at night, she hears floor boards groaning and she hopes they won't thieve her life savings in the big pot pig on the mantelpiece beside her wedding picture.

This is another area of complaint for Sue. Aunty, you should use a bank. This is crazy… and so blatant… just where someone will see it.

She's no time for such moithering. The nearest bank is in town. She'd need a crane to manhandle her there. Quite out of the question. If Sue thought for a while, she'd understand.

When Charlie perished, she went with Nana to the spiritualist, Mrs Beadle, on the Boulevard. You had to take with you some possession of the dead person. She chose his plastic comb. He'd left it on the bed in the hurry of his departure and she found it still with the black hairs twined in the teeth, and their aliveness made her cry. They were part of him, like his smell that clung to his shirts in the wardrobe, and when the smell began to fade, she plunged into despair.

So there she was with his comb that she handed to Mrs Beadle, who strafed her with a long look and then slid into a trance, her eyelids fluttering.

"Yes, yes," she said. "There's someone waiting to contact you… says he's waiting on the other side… died in a disaster… yes, something's coming through… at sea."

Dot went cold and her arms prickled with goose pimples. Charlie was over there.

Every week she went with Nana to sit in that upstairs room with trawler men's widows and old women adrift without their husbands.

Nana knew lots of old lore to make the hairs rise on the back of your neck. She'd see a seagull swooping and mewing and she'd say, "Yes, there he goes…"

"Who goes?" she asked.

"Oh, it's the soul of dead trawler men … might be your Charlie, he's watching you."

Even now as Dot lumbers back into the house, she hears the scraking and shrieking of a gull, looks up and glimpses his great yellow beak and the white waft of his wings, and she thinks, "Aye, there he is, my Charlie."

Early evening and she hears the stutter of stilettos on pavers and laughter from people making for the Queens and the Duke round the corner, for a good night on the beer. The air ripples with excitement and the scents of body sprays and perfume – it used to be hair spray. Dot dreams herself back into those nights when anything might happen and her body quivered and glowed with longing.

She's in this dream when there's a knock at the door. She hauls herself out of her chair and totters to answer the summons. It takes her a while to release the chain and unlock the Yale and the other lock which Sue has insisted she must have installed. They're nobut a bloody nuisance, she's told her niece. Takes me half an hour to get the flamin' door open!

"Wait on," she mutters, "I'm coming."

Puffing, she drags the door open and confronts a young chap. She decides he looks shifty because his eyes grasshopper about.

"Hiya," he says, "I've been looking for my aunty, she's supposed to live round here."

"Aunty? What's her name?"

"Annie."

"Annie what?"

He hesitates.

"You must know her name, lad," Dot says and fixes him with a beady eye.

At that moment somebody barges past her, almost knocking her flat. The chap on the doorstep has moved into a long and complicated story about how he doesn't know his aunty's surname.

Before Dot can react, the person who charged past her, pushes by holding her piggy bank. She stands speechless, gazing after the figure. The other chap has vaporized. In a daze she closes the front door, hobbles back to her armchair and sits down. She becomes aware of somebody scrabbling with a key in the lock and the door opens.

"Aunty Dots, you didn't even have the door locked. Anybody could walk in," Sue says.

"They just have," Dot says.

"What do you mean?"

"I've been robbed."

"Just what I always said would happen. What have they taken? Oh yes..." Her eyes leap to the mantelpiece, "I knew it. Are you all right? Here, I'd better make you a cuppa... must phone the police. What happened?"

Sue fettles around and Dot listens to the sound of her voice wittering and worrying, and finds herself smiling.

"Do you know," Dot bursts out, "he was as close to me as you are and he'd hair black as coal and the bluest eyes you ever saw."

Sue looks shocked. "But he robbed you, Aunty, he robbed you... and he'll be back. They always come back… and there are all these druggies living round about. The sooner you're out of here and the better."

Dot sips her tea and dunks a rich tea biscuit in it. She won't tell Sue because this is her secret. She doesn't care if the young man breaks in again… after all, he is Charlie re-born, not a seagull this time, but a young man, Charlie with his hair black as freshly laid tarmac and eyes so blue and hot they burn you up…

Sue is on the phone to the police, "Aunty you'll have to give a description of the man," she says.

A policeman arrives, who looks about twelve, "Now, love," he says, "Can you tell me what this man looked like?"

"Oh yes," Dot says, "he had straggly brown hair and was little and thin."

The policeman writes painful notes in his reporter's book. She embellishes her description still further and grins inwardly.

OLD SCORES

It's a bad day for John's knees. Old Bill from the gym reckons the weather plays a part in the severity of your arthritis. Maybe the cold wet spring is the culprit. If he sits down on a couch, he gets a jolt of pain when he tries to rise; makes him feel ancient, done for. The GP isn't much help, dishes out tablets that upset your stomach. The gym is the answer. Yes, you just have to keep moving.

As he climbs onto a static exercise bike, he stares out at the pond. A whole gaggle of ducks comes sweeping over the trees to glide down onto the water. He marvels at the way they move. "Bet they don't get arthritis," he thinks.

He's not been pedalling away long, before he becomes aware of a huge chap hauling himself onto one of the big bikes. Normally at this gym people call out greetings to one another, it's all very matey, and he likes that, and because it's a therapeutic place there are folks with all sorts of injuries. He's four bikes away from the big feller so he doesn't look at him or call out. Something holds him back, but John does take a sideways peek at the man after he's been biking for fifteen minutes, and is puffing and sweating. It's that prat Graham Walworth; nobody else had such a Desperate Dan jaw on them. John decided to just blank him.

Well away from the bikes, John installs himself on the leg extension. He'll do three reps of twenty-five on this. He has to stifle a groan as he raises his legs and the bar moves up. His thighs ache. The prat is still on the bike. Will he have noticed him? Nah, he'll be too full of himself, but you never know. Bloody Graham Walworth, Wally, who ran the Department with an iron hand and was forever on the prowl, snooping after you, watching what time you arrived or left. Ridiculous when you think of it – a grown man having to creep downstairs in the hope of escaping before Wally pounced. Sometimes Jack Frith was there too and they'd be choking with laughter. It made you behave like ten year olds...

But it wasn't just stuff like that – no, it got a lot darker than Wally trying to catch you out. The worst was he ensured you couldn't be promoted in any way. Every attempt you made was knocked back. Wally being so well in with the Principal, the Wicked Queen, Deidre Shaw, meant that he could feed her all sorts of muck about who he thought would be best for the job, and who he considered no-hopers.

Everybody said Wally and Deidre were having an affair. She'd wear these black, tailored suits and the skirt had a slit up the side practically to the thigh, and when she sat down, you'd see this great slice of shiny flesh and you'd have to look away and pretend you were unaware. Powerful women can be very confusing, because they send out so many conflicting signals.

There were always feuds in progress that generally erupted in the summer term, when everyone was fed up and boggle-eyed with marking, and the registers had to be done. If Wally suspected someone was not getting down to it fast enough, he'd send for them and there'd be a showdown in his room. He had to be meddling.

He moves onto the leg press and adjusts it for himself. He's set the resistance on 10, but pushing against the metal plate takes all his strength. A burning pain stretches its tentacles into his thigh and makes him gasp. He's got problems. Arthritis isn't curable, you have to live with it, the doctor said, and by 'live with it' he means endure it.

John can't help having a neb round to see if he can spot Wally's next move. He's still on the exercise bike and he's obviously struggling. "Serves the bastard right," John thinks. "He had it coming." What goes around comes around, is Mandy's favourite saying. Funny to think they've been married thirty-eight years. Of course he's never believed that people get paid back for their nastiness – it hasn't been anything he's ever noticed. The unpleasant brutes generally thrive and do better than anyone else. Seeing Wally cut down to size gives him a feeling of satisfaction, almost a warm glow – and in this instance Mandy has proved right.

"How's it going, John?" Lindsay, a wide blonde on the next machine, asks.

"The knees are fighting back!" He gives a splutter of laughter.

"Oh dear. I'm having an off day as well."

He's never been the sort to attend a gym but it seems to be the only way to stave off creeping decrepitude. He glances round. The usual clutch of heart-attack survivors clomp away on the treadmills or cycle on the static bikes, whilst discussing the latest match and who's likely to win the cup. They have to concentrate on 'cardio'. He never heard the word prior to his entering the gym world.

A couple of young bucks are having a crazy session on the arc trainers, but most of the punters are like himself, oldies and middle aged. They're beginning to feel the effects of a life time of punishing their bodies, or just ignoring them.

Usually at the gym he flops into a pleasant lulled state and stares out of the window at the pond and the Canada geese and the odd swan now and again, and the lines of dog walkers making for the park. He doesn't have to think. But today everything has changed.

He can't retire to his comfort zone.

Wally's presence poisons the air. It looks as though the trainer is explaining something to him about the static bike.

All right, he might have been five minutes late; he's never been very good at timing, but the day he found Wally asking the hairdressing apprentices what time he usually arrived to give his General Studies class, he thought he would explode. His cheeks blazed with fury and he wanted to charge straight to Wally's room and let him have it. He managed to control himself until break time, but then rage did impel him to Wally's room on the seventh floor. Jenny, Wally's secretary, prevented him from taking the matter further. "Come on, John, leave it. He's in a bad mood. Been biting everybody's head off... expect he's had a row with his wife! Have a mug of chocolate and a chocolate bickie, that'll calm you down. This is not worth it."

John's knees burn and ache deep in the bones. One of the usuals, the man on two sticks, levers himself in. When you see people like that, you can't help but feel ashamed – you've nothing really to complain about. A bit of pain perhaps, but you can't call it major. After all you can still walk.

What could have happened to Wally? Was that stroke damage? Could be... one of his arms seems useless as well. Must have got sent here by the hospital or his GP.

Greetings from a woman called Karen, who's had two knee replacements and always runs on the treadmill although the doctors have warned her it could be disastrous. She is the type who won't give in... you have to admire such obsessiveness.

He buckles his feet into the rower after adjusting the resistance to the major level, which never seems very heavy. According to Alan, one of the veterans, in the past the machines were serviced regularly but for a long time now nobody has bothered about them. What the consoles register may well be quite false.

He tries to sink into his dream of being in a long-boat sculling up the Humber, or being a Norseman steering his craft through turbulent seas. He can feel the powerful pounding of the waves and smell the brine fizzing on his cheeks. But the bile he feels at the sight of Wally won't let him concentrate on anything else.

The having to report daily to Wally's office on time to show that he had arrived was the most demeaning part of it. He'd be standing in the secretary's room, plastic carrier bag in hand, gasping after having scurried up seven flights of stairs, because the lifts were stuck and if he delayed, he'd not be there on the dot. Why didn't he tell Wally to go to hell, or simply take no notice and carry on as normal? All right, he was a bit erratic about timing, always had been. He wasn't good at the details of things, whereas Wally vacuumed up details. In science there were things to prove, concrete matters, nothing a bit smudged, open to other interpretations. Wally as he used to be, with his straight black hair that flopped over his forehead, and his gold rimmed spectacles, looked like a Mafia boss. He never seemed to take off his white lab coat, and the careful line of the black moustache and his narrow lips added to the general impression of toughness. He was no absent-minded, kindly professor.

Treadmill next. Sean has told him not to run, running can injure his knees still further. He must limit himself to power-walking: striding out whilst swinging his arms. He has to keep his gaze on a fixed point outside the window so that he won't lose his balance.

Lately he's become what he can only call 'doddery'. This can happen to you as you age, he's read. As a younger person you never think of these details. Oh, yes, you hear how so and so fell over, broke his/her pelvis, got pneumonia and died... though it seems to happen more often to women than to men.

Whilst he concentrates on keeping his stride, he forgets Wally. Fifteen minutes later he steps off the treadmill and shambles away towards the weights. There he comes face to face with Wally. Nowadays he doesn't blush, but he's shocked to feel the rush of blood to his cheeks. Wally is fighting to get a huge exercise ball across to a space by a wall. He grips his stick in one hand to support him, but he can't control his other hand.

"He's a daddy-longlegs struggling in a jar of water," John thinks. "Shall I just pretend I haven't seen him, let him drown... but it's clear I have? Should I walk by?"

"You're having a struggle," John finds himself saying.

"Hello... yes... I can't get it there."

"Right, I'll sort it," Perhaps he doesn't recognise him. They've both changed. A hell of a lot of time has whizzed by since those College days.

"Thanks very much... I say, is it John?"

John nods. "Been a long time," he says. "We're both of us showing a bit of wear and tear."

Wally grins. "You can say that again."

John manages to meet his gaze and grins back. He's sorry for the poor bastard, and there's a kind of sweetness in his face, a vulnerability he didn't have before.

"You doing all right?" Wally asks.

"Can't grumble, just the arthritis... there's thousands worse off."

"Don't suppose it's easy for you though."

"Do you ever see any of the old colleagues?" John has to ask.

"Not really... been a bit limited lately."

"What happened to Deidre Shaw?"

"She died. Got Alzheimer's and then passed away in a care home. I used to visit her there."

"Goodness..." John feels as though he's received a hefty thump to the chest. He never thought of that, but just assumed she'd be there forever in her black suit with its revealing skirt displaying those shiny thighs.

"Comes to us all," Wally sighs, and then grins. "But it's good to see you."

"Yes," John says. "I suppose we're survivors of the wreckage."

Wally smiles, "I'll be looking for you next time I'm in... what about a coffee?"

"Good idea," John says, as he departs. He feels he's got a lot to think about: everything seems off balance, out of kilter... Wally and the Wicked Queen, Deidre Shaw, have collapsed. He needs them to be the monsters, who thwarted his every move to further his career. Right now none of it seems that important.

THE COIN-OP

9.30 on a morning of high winds and driving rain, Andy, just back from dropping the kids at school, glared at the washing machine. Emma had left for work telling him to remember the wash. How could he forget it! The only little snag was that the washing machine made dirty marks on Emma's tops and the kids' sports gear.

"My Nike hoodie's ruined," Sam had moaned.

"Machine's crap, we should get a new one," David said. He was a kid with no idea about money; spoiled out of his mind. That was his problem.

They expected he would perform a magic act and lo and behold the washing machine or a new machine would make sure that all their clothes emerged pristine. He'd have a go at most machines, studying them, before carefully dismantling them, noting their layout, positioning each of their parts so he wouldn't forget the order.

Where was the machine brochure? He dragged open the top drawer of a dresser and after burrowing under piles of folded tea towels discovered it. Being a man of action he didn't want to have to sit down and read a lot of guff about what you ought to do/should already have done. He battled with an urge to act, to open the washing machine, get the top off and stare into its interior. But he forced himself to sit down at the table with the brochure and start reading. A whole lot of stuff about filters seemed important. Perhaps he could clean or change them.

In this new life since he became the one who stayed at home and did the domestic number, the days seemed to shoot past. Up to now he'd done nothing that morning but the school run, and it was cruising to lunch time. Another hour passed whilst he battled with the machine; wanted to kick it, belt it one. His head swam with blue and pink wires, microscopic connections. This was beyond him. The desire to pulverise the machine made him sweat. All that stopped him was money – they couldn't afford a new one, or even a second-hand one. Instead of laying into it, he hefted two bulging laundry bags out and humped them to the coin op a couple of streets away.

Laundrettes had become rarities. As a kid he'd seen one on every street corner and they were places where women congregated for a blether. They'd been an advance on the old wash houses that his Nana had used on Hessle Road. Nana had sent him to the laundrette on occasion and he'd sat watching his rugby and football jerseys and the legs of jeans all twizzling together and forming patterns as they whizzed round behind the giant glass eye. In those days a woman looking like a dinner lady in a blue checked overall was in charge and kept things moving. Men would disappear after putting some cash in her hand. Not today though.

Andy looked at the machine. "Morning," he said to the only customer, an older bloke, who sat reading The Daily Mail. "Hiya," the man said and returned to his paper. This was an unsupervised outfit. People puffed in, slotted cash and operated the machines themselves.

He'd not been there very long, had stowed his washing into a machine, put in his £2.40 and taken a seat before it, when a posse of kids bombed in. It soon became obvious that they hadn't come to use the coin-op, but just to create havoc. They'd taken themselves to the dryers and begun messing around with them. A little runt of a kid was even trying to climb into one. Another kid leapfrogged over the seats. They must be twagging from school and looked as though they were on something, the way their laughter cracked and their expressions seemed glazed.

He told himself he couldn't hear what was happening – it was nothing to do with him. If they wanted to behave like piss-heads then that was their business. Pity he couldn't have gone away, left his washing and collected it later. No chance now though, you'd to sit it out to the end.

A woman struggled in carrying two holdalls of damp sheets, which she wanted to put into one of the dryers.

"Can you stop fooling about, you kids," she said, as one blundered past her, causing her to flinch.

"Oh fuck off," the biggest lad said. "It dun't belong to you."

"I want to use it," she said.

"She wants to use it!" the lad mocked in a prissy voice.

"You should all be at school instead of making nuisances of yourselves in here."

Andy felt the sweat on his forehead. The kids kept up the barrage of stupid, often coarse comments and continued to caper about. Meanwhile, unable to stem the loud accompaniment, the woman installed her sheets in a dryer.

This is absolutely someone else's problem, Andy told himself again. You can't be involved with it. But the worst of it was, the woman looked weary, drudged out, as though this was the final straw. She'd told them their mams wouldn't be happy about their behaviour; weren't they ashamed? They should know better, they weren't babies. But it all appeared to have no effect, other than to make them shriller and more obscene.

The first chap had battened himself down behind his newspaper, holding the pages up so that they formed a screen.

Andy found he had clenched his fists in his hoodie pockets. He waited for the explosion.

The woman had given up trying to get the kids to clear off and was busy hauling her sheets out of the dryer and easing another lot in. She was red in the face and her mouth had drawn into a grim line. He didn't dare to look at her properly.

Two of the kids dived after each other round the machines, chortling and swearing and leaping over the woman's bags, sliding behind the seats, setting them into a judder. It was as though they were after causing the maximum amount of annoyance. He wished he'd brought a newspaper with him, anything to close him off from the scene. What would the kids get up to all day long just left to drift about wreaking havoc?

Finally when he felt hardly able to keep on sitting there and was about to leap up and seize the big lad, the ring leader got a message on his phone and with that they all disappeared. At the same time the woman zipped up her holdalls and trundled out into the rain and wind. The other machine user folded up his paper, slid it into his anorak pocket and set about laying his clean washing into a sports-bag.

"Thank God they've gone," he said. "Them kids want shootin. That's what they do to some of them street kids in where is it? Guatemala or whatever they call it. Best thing for 'em."

Andy didn't say anything at first. Fury still rippled round the laundrette; it was as though it couldn't disperse.

"I was embarrassed," Andy said, "seeing them talking to that woman like that but I knew if I started getting involve..."

"Oh yer, you can't get involved... dun't do no good – next thing you've got police on your back and it's your fault..."

"Yes," Andy said, "that's about the size of it." That set him wondering why the man was wary of the police. He'd have a story... so many stories. Something would have happened and you'd be branded for all time and there'd be no escape. And that was how it had been at the Academy when he'd been summoned by the On-Call officer to stop the commotion in Miss Pringle's classroom. There she'd been waving her arms about and shrieking, near tears. He'd had to capture that kid Smithson, who'd terrorized the staff. He'd tried to walk him to the Unit where he'd have explained about the Restorative work, only they'd never got there, because the kid had kicked him and run off...

The next thing, the Head had sent for him: Andy, I'm afraid there has been a complaint from Dwayne Smithson's mother. So there he was, suspended from teaching kickboxing in schools; mustn't work with children pending the outcome of the investigation. Now two years down the line, cleared of the case against him, told he could work in schools again, he didn't want to. He'd become afraid, always jumpy. He could see a disaster a mile off before it arose. Whereas before, he'd gone with his feelings of wanting to protect folk who couldn't defend themselves... like the woman in the coin-op... now he could sense the handcuffs biting into his wrists. No, he couldn't help them.

Shame burned in his face that he should have sat there and let the woman struggle on with the mob of kids cursing and swearing at her. Perhaps he could belt after her and apologise, but it was too late... and he'd the clean laundry to stow in the bags.

He plodded up the road home with the rain slamming into his face and he was aware of a hollow in his gut. Evidently you had to pay a heavy price for doing the right thing.

ESCAPING

Maggie watches the thundering lorries. They ride the switchback road bucking and rattling. She is surprised more accidents don't happen. Accidents skulk behind the day's trivia, always threatening to erupt. The speed limit is forty mph but most must be hitting sixty at least, as they race to catch the ferry or reach the BP refinery. Dust coats everything. She's given up wiping the outside window ledges. You would need to do them three or four times a day to keep them immaculate.

A lull – nobody in for petrol; nobody buying milk, bread, chocolate bars; too early for those knocking off work or stray school kids, or girls and women with clutches of screaming bairns visiting the prison up the road.

The sky is a curious margarine colour. She feels a sudden rush of heat to her cheeks and goes to stand at the entrance to the shop. A dead stretch of road. Everything lower down has sunk into dereliction. The greasy spoon cafe is boarded up; the newsagent's has gone out of business; the dodgy club closed down. About two years ago a woman got raped and murdered on this strip.

You wouldn't walk down here at night, not in this area where nobody lives and there is just the prison and the disused cemetery, and a timber yard. Up beyond that is the maternity hospital at the top of a long drive. On the other side of the road lies the vestigial dockland. Of course, the fishing industry is finished. She studies the giant crane arms poking above the embankment and wonders what lies over there. In the same way she wonders when she passes that grim redbrick fortress daily, but never gets to see the interior… so many hidden insides.

She can never let things alone, but must ferret away at them. When she was a kid, she and her best mate, Sandra, climbed into a disused building. Some said it had been a workhouse; somebody else said a mosque. Pages written in a black twirly script drifted along a paved walkway. Maggie picked up the sheets but couldn't understand them and that made it even more of a mystery. Being inside wasn't enough…

Joe, her husband, says, "Why can't you leave things be? Inspector Rhodes, that's you. I don't understand why you have to poke your nose in."

If only sometimes she could take a ferry trip over to Holland or Belgium – it needn't be far. Of course Joe won't; being a workaholic he never leaves the garage. Sometimes chunky foreigners in leather coats and carrying calf holdalls pass on foot, chattering in unknown languages. Germans and Scandinavians, zipped into blue anoraks, rucksacks and sleeping bags strapped to their backs, plod past, all trekking from the ferry terminal to the town. She often feels like running after them.

Once a young chap came off his motorbike outside the garage and was run over by a lorry. She saw the tyre print on his face.

Another time she saw a police car chase, cars dodging like crazy up the road, away into the distance, leaving violent trails behind.

Brad outmanoeuvres the Mondeo trying to sneak up. He growls into acceleration and closes up to the lorry in front. Insane drivers, he thinks and curses. Then the steering skews oddly and he struggles to keep the van on the road. The Mondeo swerves past as Brad loses speed. Bastard! he mutters. Better pull over. There's a garage on the left. He signs and lollops in, flinging out of the van, and bangs along to stand before the bonnet, where he glares at the front tyres. Massive puncture, tyre shredded on nearside. He steams with irritation. Waste of money, waste of time. No spare in the boot… well, he hasn't counted on this. Have to buy a new tyre… a place like this is bound to rob you… bound to.

He strides up to the woman standing in the doorway. "Got a puncture – got anybody here to repair that?" He points at the tyre, watching the woman's face. She stares at him blankly and says if he goes into the workshop, he'll see one of the boys. Should he have to wait, he can have a coffee from the machine. If he wants.

"Yer, right," he says, and crashes off in search of the lads. Might be able to get them to repair it, worth a try. Of course they'll push him towards a new tyre but you have to watch 'em. They're all thieves.

Two youths in blue boiler suits emerge blinking, like tortoises ambling out of hibernation. A right pair of dodos, he thinks.

"Now then, get us that repaired, will you… jump to it!"

They saunter to the van and gawp at the tyre. "Eh, you'll not be able to repair that," one says.

"Naw it's good and gone," the other says with satisfaction.

"Get it off and let's see!" Brad instructs.

They look dubious and then one departs and returns lugging the car jack. He pumps away on the lever and the van rises. They work the tyre off whilst Brad fumes and gnaws his lower lip.

"Naw, look at that – shredded – can't do owt with that… well, it'ud be dangerous."

"Not legal..." the other one comes in.

Brad hesitates but finally gives in. "Go on then – got any remoulds?"

"Naw, don't do remoulds."

"Fuckin' hell, what do you do?"

They agree on a new tyre eventually and one goes off to fetch it. Brad lurches off to pay. The woman still stands peering out.

"Not much trade here then – not surprised the way you rob the punters blind."

"How do you mean?" she says.

"Could have got this repaired at any decent garage – instead, they force you to buy a new 'un."

"Is that right?" she says. "Want a coffee?"

He pauses, cut off mid-grouch. "Oh, go on then."

"Milk and sugar?"

He nods. She presses various buttons on the machine and hands him a plastic cup. He sips and forgets his irritation.

"I suppose nothing much happens along here," he says, wanting to prise some reaction from her.

"You could say that – but sometimes... I mean, I've worked here for years like... there was the time this prisoner escaped. You know the prison's just along there..."

"Yes," he says and suspends his drinking, shocked into watching her face.

"Well, I used to look at it... always do... the big wall and the razor wire and everything... because you wonder... anyway. It was afternoon like and I was out at the pumps. Wasn't self-service then. He climbed over the wall and somehow escaped."

She stands by the cash register, her face in a flash come to life, pink now and her eyes cobalt blue – he's used that colour in his pictures – his favourite blue, excitable eyes in a flat face. She gives him a receipt. But he remains standing there, looking at her, the plastic cup in his hand.

"And I saw him run round the corner and he was panting. Then the police cars swooped down and all these officers... it was terrible... it made me feel ill... like hunting at animal."

Brad is now in that afternoon. He hears the breath stuttering in his throat as he scrambles up the wall and gazes down the long drop into the cemetery. He has to chance it. Whoosh. The air gusts past his ears. He plummets and his leg twists. Pain shoots up him like a flame. His head goes hot, then icy. He hears a crack – bones, ligaments? They'll be after him.

Stumbling amongst the memorials to the long dead, he tries to fight down the rush of nausea. The bitter pungency of crushed couch grass, dock leaves and nettles stings his nostrils. He must get to the road. He doesn't know this city. He arrived here in a dog-box with darkened windows and has no knowledge of its contours. London is his world… Euston Road. He could have dived away there and found a bolt hole no problem.

He's out of the cemetery, crouches by the wall and then speeds along the front, turns right and pelts up a slight incline. There is pain with every movement. He has to halt at the bridge and leans there, panting and vomits over it and watches sour gobs of half-masticated chips and greasy fritters plopping on gravel and blowing back in long strings to festoon the bridge supports. The sirens scream. He turns, slumped against the parapet, and watches the jam-sandwich police cars honing in on him. A navy-blue posse thunders up the road.

Hands claw at him. The shock of them vibrates through his body. They snap handcuffs on him and bundle him into the police car. The whole road has been blocked off, he registers with wry amusement that seeps through the pain.

Escape to nowhere, he thinks, just the start of a long string of nick years. He didn't return to this city until several prison sentences later – by then doing the 'biggy', the 'A' man with an eighteen stretch. You wouldn't escape now over the new electrified fence and the dogs would bite your fucking leg off…

The woman's eyes burn. "Yes," she says. "It was a funny thing that – I often wonder about that man – what happened to him I mean. Of course this is all years ago… but I never forgot."

"No," he says.

"Nothing like that has ever happened since."

"And it won't," he says. "Well, ta for the coffee – I'm off now."

He and the woman exchange a long look and then he shoulders out to his pick-up. He is still in that time twenty-five, twenty-six years ago… no, longer than that even, much longer. He shoots into the far past, takes in Approvie, Detention Centre, Borstal… Maximum Security nick. Spaces in between: moments in ringed cars with a shooter; little bank jobs in balaclavas, armpits steaming, adrenalin pumping, bowels bubbling. Girls with lacquered hair still and high as hay-stacks and smelling of scent and soap, blonde legs, stiletto heels like blades, fags nipped in pale fingers between red nails.

He moves with the big boys in sharp suits whose hair shines as black as eels and who operate in gangs. Excitement nearly stops his heart. He catapults from one adventure into another – all going, going and the cash spilling from his pockets, the days churning, the adrenalin sparking.

Blonde Chrissy is his lover for a while. At the start of a seven stretch she comes in a fur coat to the closed visit and standing behind the mesh reinforced glass, she opens her coat. Nobody sees except him that she is totally naked inside the garment. She smiles.

"Just helping out," she calls though the glass.

Chrissy has been long since lost in all these years. The women couldn't wait. By the time you were on the out again, they had found another true love.

He thinks of Smudger, Bobby, and Wilky. Smudger is currently going a seventeen stretch for drugs in the eighties. Wilky is dead. Shot in a pub.

The van rumbles and whines along the pitted road. He gets a feel of his pad in the old days: screws' keys tinkling along the outside wall; pad doors slamming; the stench of shit in the piss pots; pigeons whoo-whooing on the window sill, blurry shapes roosting; metal food trays, custard slopping onto chip-compartment; covert information slipping out the side of your mouth. A daily battle, a throbbing purpose, all straining towards THE OUT, a date ringed in red on a mental calendar.

Soon he trundles through the city centre with the van hiccupping now and then and him cursing. He knows this city as well as his own history now. His gaze misses nothing. Up by a line of prissy 1930s semis, white paint and coach lamps; now away out to the select residential area devoid of chip shops and take-away outlets, where big modern mock Georgian houses squat behind pillared fronts. He takes a sharp right turn and chugs up a drive between high laurel bushes. Inge's great mellow brick mansion hides behind a Wellingtonia and several spruces. On sunny days he often stands for a secret moment breathing in the dark, aromatic scent of pines in sunlight. Now he goes straight to the back door.

"Good, you're back – you're late. I was starting to worry," Inge says. "I've just made tea… come on."

She pours jasmine tea into shell white cups and turns to smile at him.

They are in the conservatory amid monsteras, rubber plants, lemon trees and flowering jasmine. The strange stark perfume of the flowers hits his nostrils. He thumps down in a black leather lounger and sighs.

Late sunlight pours through the glass and falls on the serrated monstera leaves. The rubber plant presses thick oval foliage towards the roof, and where the leaves are about to unfold, pink phallic pointers show. He mumbles about the puncture, robbers etc, but his attention fixes on the plants. Gradually he relaxes and bites into Inge's cucumber sandwiches; the crusty brown bread sooths.

"Happened near the nick," he tells her.

"Oh, right – look at this," she says, pointing to a piece in the day's newspaper. He focuses on the mug shot of a middle-aged man: Bobby. Someone has gunned Bobby down in a Soho street. Drugs are thought to be involved.

Brad sits quite still, staring at the jasmine tea, stunned with the pity of it.

"He never managed to escape," Brad says. "Even when you're on the out, you haven't escaped... not if you stay down there."

He remembers the pull of the early months: would he go back to London, to the lads, and be drawn in? All so easy. But there was Inge, Inge the artist, who visited the prison. Inge teased out curly metallic shapes, and saw wonders in a chunk of drift wood, or a piece of stone. So he didn't go back to the streets of his childhood and he has lived with Inge in her enchanted castle, where they can't find him... but sometimes like today, the past will tug at him, and he will feel its vibrations, but that's all...

To Maggie, the stranger's face looks as though it has had a tractor driven across the forehead. The cheek bones are high, gristly knots and the slit eyes don't miss a trick. A Slav face, a face from Outer Mongolia. A face that has seen things, seen too much. The face makes her talk, spill her secrets. As he stomps away with his peculiar boxer's walk, she is still in the day of the man running from the prison pursued by the navy-blue mob.

I could have escaped, she thinks, and her face throbs with heat, her nostrils dry. She coughs. I could have gone with Larry...

Larry was her ballroom dancing partner; Larry of Monday evenings and the glassy dance floor: palms touching; his hand, low down on her back; spin-turns, an exquisite pivoting. He, and she in a frothy pink gown, caught in a mirrored wall. He had a face like a blade, a pale shining face and hair slicked back with Brylcreme. He was married, of course he had to be married, like she was – just.

It was all set, all arranged for that Monday evening. She packed her case, dithering with terror. Everything about the day rushed at her, pounced on her. Her skin became too thin. She was crazy with longing at the thought of escaping with him.

Mid-afternoon and she stood at the pumps, trying to concentrate. She couldn't remember how many gallons the motorist wanted.

Escape. The prisoner in his faded blue cotton trousers and striped shirt pounded up the road... only he didn't escape. She couldn't watch as the police cars sealed off the road, instead she stumbled into the kiosk and messed with the cash register. Tears scorched the back of her throat.

It might go all wrong. She struggled with guilt, seeing Joe's face when he would find the note – the note was ready in her handbag. Standing in the kiosk, sick with suspense, she followed the man in blue, imagined them taking him away... And then... no, she couldn't leave Joe, she couldn't walk out... but she could, she could make things happen.

The hands of the clock flurried round. Her heart banged, her head swam, her ears pounded. She twirled on the glassy ballroom floor, or sank under the pressure of Larry's hot wet mouth, as they strained between the gear lever in the front seat of his Avenger.

She doesn't really know why she didn't run away with Larry that evening – it was something to do with the feeling that came on her, the realization that there could be no escape, as she waited by the pumps.

A blue mini pulls up on the forecourt and she sees her daughter, Sharon, getting out.

"I'll have to ask Dad to look at this," Sharon says, "funny clanking noise in the engine."

Sharon disappears into the workshop and emerges a while later with Joe. Maggie watches his boiler-suited back, notes the slightly sunken angle of his neck as he bends over the bonnet of Sharon's car. She has not noticed that before and she is caught in an almost suffocating need to rush out and hug him.

SAILING NEAR THE ROCKS

Anne watches her husband's face as he takes the call, and her chest feels tight.

"It's Mark," he says. "He's coming round."

"But what's the matter?"

"He just said, I'm in trouble, that's all."

"What sort of trouble?"

"Didn't say."

"I wonder if he and Helen have split up or something…"

"Look, Anne, for goodness sake, you don't know and no point in speculating endlessly. There's no reason why it has to be anything like that. I can't imagine why you said it."

"But trouble…"

"Let's just wait."

Anne hates situations like this, where you are stranded with insufficient information, but knowing that something unpleasant is pending. Conrad deals in facts, never anticipating the outcome of things, whereas she mulls over possibilities, and by the time she is confronted by whatever it is, she isn't so flummoxed by it.

An hour later the front door judders. Anne scoops in air and tries to smile in readiness. The lounge door eases open. She always knows when Mark is in the house.

"Hi," he says, and sinks down on the sofa. Anne can see from his closed expression that he isn't really aware of them, but preoccupied with whatever has brought him there.

"What about a drink, Love. Tea, coffee?"

"Oh, don't worry about that. I'm all right."

"A wine or a beer or something?" Conrad asks.

"Red wine, Dad, please."

Whilst Conrad wanders off to fetch an opener and select a bottle of wine, Anne finds glasses and continues to smile, though she is aware throughout of Mark's fiddling with his phone and his distracted glances. He generates waves of anxiety. Whatever is disturbing him must be serious.

Conrad in his deliberate way is still deciding on the bottle and digging out the opener.

"You pressing the grapes, Dad?" Mark says.

|||

Anne gives an embarrassed laugh. There's a silence. She can't ask him how he is because it's obvious. "Is Helen all right?" she manages.

"I think so."

"Oh good." What a peculiar answer – why did he 'think' so? With Mark you can never enquire very deeply; everything has to be kept on a superficial level. Perhaps she should ask after Helen's parents, though she has only met them once and that was at the wedding.

"Right, here we are!" Conrad appears with the wine.

Anne shakes her head, "I'll make a coffee in a minute." She watches as Mark takes a long swallow. She doesn't like the way he's almost glugging it down. Half has already disappeared. Let him just tell them what it is. Anne feels the smile setting on her face, so that her skin is tight and stretched.

"Okay," he starts, "you'd better hear this first from me, because there's going to be a lot more of it later."

Anne lets her face ease out. No use now to pretend. Smiling would inappropriate. Has he killed someone?

"I'm in trouble… dead trouble. It's all over something that has happened…"

So what is it… let him just say it out? Anne finds it difficult to remain seated, watching him struggling. He swigs his wine, finishes it and holds his glass out for a fill up.

"It's to do with the school."

Oh God, this is bound to be very serious… has he slapped a child? Hurt someone? Everything closes in. She wishes she'd got a mug in her hands. She can't look at him.

"Ah yes," Conrad says, "the school…"

"I'm accused of improper conduct with a pupil."

"And is it true?" she blurts out, feeling the heat shoot up her neck. This is the last thing she expected. It has never entered her head that he should be a… a paedophile… what an ugly word… the worst thing he could have done.

"What do you think?"

"I've no idea," she says, "though I can't imagine this is something you would do."

"Quite… but anyway, I've been suspended, pending police investigations, and there'll be a court case. I expect the press will get at it and you'll be seeing my face slapped on the front page – 'Teacher abuses Pupil' – and I could get sent to prison."

"But they can't," Anne squeaks. "I mean you've not done it, have you, and they can't do this to an innocent person."

"You'd be surprised what they can do."

"I'm very sorry, son," Conrad says.

"But why are they accusing you, Mark?" Anne says.

"Troublemakers." He continues to knock-back the wine and stares into space.

"How is Helen taking it?" Anne asks.

"She's gone home to her parents for the weekend."

"Upset, I suppose... can't be easy. What does she make of it?" Anne isn't satisfied; feels nothing has really been explained, somewhere there's a missing key to what has happened. "Who made the allegations?"

"Does it matter?"

"Well, I just thought it might help, but don't tell me if you don't want to." She has obviously irritated him by her persistence and she can feel him bridling.

"What shall you do with yourself while you're not at work," Conrad says.

"Go to the gym... it's no use sitting at home and moping."

"Very sensible. That's the idea!"

"I'm going to get on with supper," Anne says. "You'll stay?"

"Thanks, Mum, might as well."

By this time he is well down the bottle of wine. He certainly won't be able to drive his car. She expects she'll have to ferry him back.

Whilst she checks the roasting chicken and the potatoes and makes gravy, she examines what she has just heard. She isn't satisfied and guesses there is more in this than Mark has revealed. To be accused of misconduct he must have done something to make people suspicious. Of course he will have to sue. She will suggest that over the meal, ask whether he has got a solicitor on the case – it needs fighting. He has nothing to lose; after all this is about his integrity, his future, his livelihood.

Finally they are sitting down to eat. Anne, glancing across the table at her son, thinks he looks a lot older than twenty-three, more like forty-three. There is a greyish tone to his cheeks and his hair hangs in greasy strands. Somewhere he had lost his young, fit, athletic self. She has always been very proud of him; he had a first at Uni, and got his post in the prestigious private school against stiff competition. Surely this whole business won't come to anything. But what if it does? How will she be able to lift her head, look people straight in the eye, and say, Yes, our son was dismissed from teaching for unsuitable conduct... is in prison?

"What are you going to do?" she says, when they've reached the homemade apple pie and cream stage.

"Don't know… no plans."

She wants to ask if Helen will stand by him, but she can't. The fact that Helen is visiting her parents just now does not bode well. She supposes it will depend on the nature of the 'misconduct'. The word could denote anything. The worst will be some sort of sexual misdemeanour… and with whom would that be… boys, girls? Anne's neck and chest continue to burn.

By the time she carries the tray with the coffee cups and cafetiere into the lounge, Conrad is describing some football incident during England's last game against France. She can see from Mark's expression that he isn't listening. He's away somewhere in his head. Conrad won't know how to cope with any further revelations from Mark. He can't stand heavy emotional stuff and usually tries to pretend it isn't happening.

She pours the coffee and hands it out. Mark looks exhausted. "Do you want to stay the night?" she says. "The bed in your old room is aired… you can go home in the morning." To her surprise he takes up her offer and the wire of tension seems to relax. He lolls back in an armchair.

Dead on 10.50pm Conrad stands up and announces he must get some sleep. Mark, though slack with tiredness, shows no sign of going up to bed and Anne feels too alert and apprehensive to sleep. She listens to her husband's measured footfalls on the stairs and then she turns to Mark. "Your dad's a creature of habit," she says.

"You can say that again."

At 11.30pm she makes a pot of tea. They have continued to chat about trivialities. And then as she passes him the mug of tea, he says, "It's all because of Emily."

"Oh," she mutters, to show she is listening, but is loathe to interrupt the flow.

"She was in my tutor group… very bright… the cleverest. Gave her some private coaching after school." He concentrates on the mug of tea, and silence stretches between them. The ramifications of this are going to be very serious. She knows he is aware of it now… it will surely mean prison and being on the Sex Offenders' Register. But he would have known that at the time, realized the dangers… after all, he is an adult, Emily the child, and he is responsible for her safety. If things were reversed and she was the girl's mother, she would be filled with fury that her young daughter has been preyed on.

"How has it come to light?" Anne asks.

"Her mother read her diary and saw texts she's sent me on her phone. Her parents got onto the school straight away."

"But they can hardly accuse you of misconduct for coaching the girl…"

"It wasn't just that."

Anne feels how her skin freezes now. She can't imagine that Helen, his wife of a year, will be very interested in standing by him. Who would want to be married to a paedophile? He has betrayed her trust and ruined this young girl's life too. She has to stifle an urge to register her complete disapproval… well, it is more than that, it is utter disgust.

"I never intended to get involved… it just happened."

It enrages her to hear him talking like this, as though he is incapable of controlling himself. She wants to tell him that he has just been indulging his vanity… a young girl is infatuated by him, so he responds, as it strokes his ego. This is my son, a seducer of a young girl. And what about Helen? How can she cope with it?

"This is going to be very serious," Anne says, trying to choke down her anger and horror at what he has done.

"I told you, didn't I?" He groans and puts his head in his hands.

She wants to say, yes and you've brought it all on yourself, you're not stupid, you knew what you were doing. But something halts her.

She was twenty-two, a German teacher, in her first post, not long married to Conrad, who, as a nautical engineer, worked away for months at a time. Could they possibly put up this fifteen-year old German boy, Jurgen, for four weeks, as he needed to brush up his spoken English and no family could be found to take him. During the day he could attend school. She had grumbled but agreed, although she didn't fancy having this unknown boy around all the time… it wouldn't have been so bad had Conrad been at home.

His beautiful blond face and speedwell blue eyes shocked her. On first meeting he inclined his head to shake her hand and clicked his heels. It made her feel grown up. She could no longer be this crazy girl still dallying with student days. He saw her as the Hausfrau and expected her to act the woman of the house.

Every day together they walked the fifteen minute journey to and from the school; she holding her brief case, he with his backpack. He enjoyed sports, was quite athletic. Tea in the kitchen, interspersed with his very correct English, and her little corrections of it at times. She would lapse into German to explain something to him.

There was the laughter, the sharing and always his very blue eyes with their mauve veining smiling at her, joking, leading her on. And she found how she looked forward to their arrival at home in the late afternoon and his laughing queries about things he had encountered during the day's lessons. It seemed natural for him to be around all the time, and them to be together. They discussed difficult words in both languages. She got him to recite, 'Am grauen Strand am grauen Meer...' and loved the sonorousness of the lines, fell in love with his voice and his lips forming the words.

Then they were laughing at some triviality... being alone with him in the yellow brick terrace house, they were cast up on an island and beyond it nothing else existed except a sea. She didn't think of Conrad's home coming or of Jurgen's returning to his parents. Suddenly it was the Saturday morning two days before his departure.

He knocked at her bedroom door. She was up awake but still in her slithery pink and white dressing gown, naked beneath it. She let him in. What he wanted was not clear. She couldn't quite understand, told him to speak more slowly. He'd got the wrong tense, she made him repeat it. There was laughter, silliness. How it happened, she didn't know, but he chased her round the bedroom, caught her up in his arms and she was conscious of the desire in his eyes, the heat... and she knew she must pull back. This was the approach of something overwhelming. Here was a boundary she must not cross. Her flesh was heavy with longing, but her head forced her back.

She shook free of him, told him to put the kettle on, let her dress and she'd be down in a couple of minutes. He hadn't expected that, was unprepared for the abrupt reversal. She listened to him running down the stairs, and seemed to emerge from a dream. She wasn't a teenager, she was the older person, the one in charge, the teacher. It was a matter of trust, and the thought of how close she had come to abusing it made her tremble, and she sat in the warm bed room on that August morning, struggling for composure.

She looks at her son, sitting on the couch with his head bowed, and she is able to rise, walk across to him and place a hand on his shoulder. What can she say to him? This is life: there are times of temptation, moments of intense longing and desire but you must think outside and beyond them to the effect of your actions on others... only he knows that now, she can't, shouldn't verbalize it, better to leave it all unsaid.

"I don't know where this will end, Mum," he says.

"No, whatever happens, we shall stand by you."

"Thank you," he says, "The problem is, I can't get Emily out of my mind… I really love her."

Anne gazes into her son's treacle coloured eyes as he raises his head and focuses on her. She knows what that feels like; it is an ache in the pit of your stomach and in your chest. Her eyes fill with tears.

"When I was your age, already married to your Dad, I–" He has turned his head to look at her. She meets his eyes, his lashes like hers are spiked with tears. "Well – your Dad was away…"

"Anne, I've got indigestion again." Conrad has come downstairs in his dressing-gown and minus his spectacles looks cut adrift.

"They'll be in the bathroom cabinet. I'll get you something," Anne says. She gives her son a quick hug, "Are you going to call it a day?" she asks Mark.

"Might as well, Mum," Mark says getting up. "And thank you."

THE WEDDING PHOTOGRAPH

Loz's customers were mainly female: women who preferred the single life; widows; abandoned wives and partners; gay women; escapees from loveless relationships. Many of them presented him with gifts. One gave him a black plastic bin liner stuffed with her dead husband's socks.

"You will wear them, won't you?" she'd said and he'd assured her he would, though he disliked the conker-brown pairs with red stripes and the vomit-coloured acrylic ones decorated with navy-blue clocks, and he sensed the dead husband's ghost hovering over him. He would have been a bloke with a high-blood pressured face and a love of red sweaters that reflected on his cheeks.

One of his regulars, Mrs. Grey, abandoned by her partner, had a baby and four-year old Amy. "I want to climb your ladders, Loz," Amy said. He happened to turn round and discovered her following him towards the roof. Heart in his mouth, he must turn and encourage her down. In between shinning up his ladder he pulled faces at the baby and made it chortle. Amy wanted to give a skipping demonstration and then was persuaded to concentrate on drawing a picture. "You see I can't do that like you," Loz said, "Climbing a ladder is easy-peasy. Drawing isn't." As he was leaving Amy rushed up with a posy of cat mint and pink geraniums and the picture of him climbing his ladder.

When he'd finished replacing slates and tiles or sash-bars on windows; pointing chimney stacks; installing digital T.V. aerials, they'd often invite him in for a mug of tea. They'd forget he'd said tea without milk or sugar please, and hand him an evil tasting beverage bleached with full-fat milk. In the middle of a story of desertion, "Well of course I'd no idea what he was getting up to and…" he'd wrestle with the problem of how to rid himself of the noxious liquid. Saved. The doorbell tinkled. He was out of the French windows like a streaking tomcat and had tipped the tea into the border trying to avoid scalding the scarlet snapdragons.

Today he had a chimney stack to point and a gutter to renew on a semi-detached Victorian house. It stood in the middle of an 1890s terrace. He enjoyed the mellow orange brick and the unbroken line of the grey slate roofs with their original block gutter supports and fascia boards. The owner was Mrs Evelyn Brooks, a widow. He'd worked on her roof periodically over the years. Often he knew people's roofs better than their owners' faces. But Mrs. Brooks' face was one he couldn't forget. It wasn't at all pretty, looked almost haggard and crisscrossed with living, but when she smiled the lines made patterns and her eyes creased into blue diamonds. Unlike many of his other customers, she never embarked on an 'Ancient Mariner' tale. Her husband, whom Loz had never met, must have died many years ago.

Invited in once to examine a leaking bay, he had noticed a silver framed photograph of a man on the mantelpiece. The man's eyes were smoky and brooding and his black hair brushed back from a square forehead; quite a handsome, hawkish face. Had she loved him? Loz had seen many photographs of dead husbands. Sometimes they stood on bedside tables, and he glimpsed them through windows as he climbed his ladder to the roof. This one though was on public display... what did that betoken? Suppose they'd spent an unhappy life together, that she'd really hated him, but once he was no longer there, she began to love him.

As he mounted his ladder, he thought of his sister-in-law, Rebecca. She and Brian had spent their marriage snapping and sniping at each other, and she would fizz with anger as she recounted his misdeeds to her sister, Leah. And then last year Brian succumbed to a massive heart attack. Since then, to Loz's amazement, Brian had been reinvented and become the love of Rebecca's life.

But of course other women didn't hide their animosity to their dead husbands – there'd been the woman who complained, "He was always making boxes, little boxes... he'd be out in his shed making boxes..."

Were the boxes symbols of his entrapment?

Up there on the roof he could breathe, was in his enchanted territory. He saw blue tits squeezing under gaps in slates to reach their nests; wasps' nests; miniature trees flourishing in gutters. He loved the symmetry of those roofs. The crown chimney pots cut patterns in the sky. He was on a level with the sycamore billows. Gulls swooped to and fro; crows squawked. The lime trees were sticky with pollen and wasps rasped.

On this July day the baking slates burned and scalded his knees through his jeans as he laboured hour after hour. He knew most of the roofs on that terrace and had witnessed all manner of dramas whilst working on them. Through a glassed-in bay roof he'd seen a young woman playing with her children. The lodger ran a hand down her back and lifted her corn-coloured hair to drop a kiss on her neck. Thirty-five slates later the husband arrived home from work.

Up and down ladders he went, bearing cement for re-pointing chimney stacks. On the way he'd glimpse the acres of heavy, pale flesh of women dressing. Meeting them later, when he came for payment, he kept his expression neutral, strove to be matter of fact.

Late afternoon and he pressed the door bell and waited for Mrs. Brooks to appear.

"I think you'll be all right now," he said, when she stood smiling in the doorway.

"Do come in, you must be exhausted. I must give you something to drink."

She handed him a glass of chilled apple juice and he found himself unable to avoid the dark gaze of the man in the silver frame.

"I see you're looking at my husband Henry," she said.

"He was very handsome."

"Yes," she said, "and when he died, I thought I'd never survive it. Little things… I couldn't get myself to prepare meals for one… I simply couldn't eat. It took a long time. I was in a fog…" She seemed to be trying to drag herself out of the past. "Now," she said, "I've decided I must down size. I'm selling up – it's a wrench, but I have to. I wondered if you'd like this picture?"

From an adjoining room she produced a nondescript print of a hunt – it looked more like a page from some 'Hare and Hounds' magazine – not that he knew anything about such things.

"It was his favourite picture – he kept it in his study, facing the desk… well, I can't take everything with me. What do you think, Loz?"

"Very kind of you, Mrs. Brooks." The frame would be useful anyway.

On reaching home, he realized that Leah must be still out at one of her classes. He carried the picture to his hut, and with care ran his penknife round the back of it to ease it out of its frame. He laid the glass on his work bench. The print came away to reveal a wedding photograph: the groom clearly Henry, the bride not Evelyn, but a much smaller, curvy girl.

He sat for a while on the garden seat in the falling dusk. The air was thick and his T-shirt stuck to him. A strange day… but the gutters had gone all right…unsettling. Leah called to him from the back door and he saw the glow in her face and he wondered…

STRANGE MEETING

The snow whirled and fluttered like so many butterflies' wings, stuck to Eleanor's eyelids and melted on her cheeks. What had seemed magical at the outset began to change. The wind drove dense flurries straight at her. Buffet after buffet the white mass came on. Once she slipped, almost tumbled, but righted herself with a judder. She must take care – this was the sort of scenario where you could break wrists, knees, or your pelvis. Every winter the orthopaedic department at the Infirmary bulged with middle aged women waiting to be treated.

Only 3.30pm but you could imagine it was 6.30 or later. A gloom shrouded everywhere. Once past the line of houses there was nothing, just a dual carriageway to negotiate – scary with such poor visibility, though there'd not been any cars for some time, just the heavy silence. Strange how when it snowed in the night, you'd wake to a stillness, even the sound of passing vehicles was muffled. Even before you opened the curtains, you knew how it would be.

On she plodded, slithering and sliding, longing to be home. A pot of tea and two well toasted crumpets swimming with honey in front of the gas fire... what bliss! The butter and the honey melted into the pocked surface. You had to make sure that it was crisp and not soggy so that it held the butter. Shoes off, coat off... oh, the pleasure of being in a warm house. If you concentrated on heat sufficiently, you were meant to be able to generate it...

The wind blasting in her face made her struggle to breathe and reduced her speed to a shamble. If only she wasn't one of those adenoidal people who must walk with their mouths open!

February was always the worst month. Davy took off in February; it was the seventeenth. This must be some omen. A new post... yes, moving to Leeds; we must sell up. In line for a chair... success after all these years of hard work. Davy, a jumpy, daddylong legs of a man, tended not to look people in the face. With acquaintances his gaze strayed over their shoulders or clung round their knees, only now he couldn't even meet her eyes. He talked up the promotion promise, the move to the Mecca of the North, his voice wired up by forced enthusiasm that didn't reach his eyes. Icy draughts petrified her shoulders and they strained up to her ears. And then he told her; "Look Eleanor," (Not Ellie – so this meant it was serious and she never liked it when he pronounced 'Eleanor' in that tone)

"I've been feeling for some time that I need to find myself, get away. I realize I'm depressed being with you here."

Those words 'find myself' had been a code that she couldn't crack, until later after he'd left, and she had to sell that handsome house with its mysterious garden.

She continued blundering along, her middle screwed up with rage and despair. Why did you have to cherish traumas and disappointments? Why couldn't you shed them like chrysalises did their skin?

You could die out here in this white wilderness. A grip on her arm travelled through her in shock waves. She tottered, almost keeled over. Her heart thundered. What was this? Serial killer, rapist... you read sensational accounts all the time and always pitied the victims, visualizing their last moments of despair. Nobody was going to rescue them. The best thing was to die at the start, rather than have a protracted struggle before being strangled and raped.

But the hand yanked on her bag strap in an attempt to wrest it from her. So that was it, he wanted her bag. A mugging! She'd often heard of people being mugged. Mugged was such an ugly word.

She hugged her arm into her side, trying to keep her bag squeezed there, but the claw applied more pressure. Her feet slid on the pavement. He wasn't going to get it. All her life she'd let things be wrenched out of her grasp... her husband, her home, her comfy leather Chesterfield... She heard herself gasping. He snorted. What did the brute look like? She swung round, wanting to kick him, but he twisted her wrist. The pain burned up her arm. She still clung on. They grasped at each other like two wrestlers.

There was a crash and she saw his bike fall to the ground. Her assailant halted and turned his head. Her hand fell back and she felt snow melting on her face and neck. In that second she got a look at him – gone-off milk skin, sharp cheek bones, a rattish nose. It was the lad who'd annoyed the life out of her.

The tugging stopped abruptly, the wrestling ceased. Eleanor stared into eyes the colour of scummy washing up water. The eyes shot wide at first with amazement and then they crinkled and the mouth split with laughter to expose a few teeth like remnants of a bomb blasted building.

"Eh, didn't know it was you, Miss – sorry about that..."

What was his name? He was older now. Then he'd been hyperactive, couldn't concentrate, but would set the others off with his inane laugh. And he'd truanted. She had been supposed to follow up his absences, but she hadn't wanted to know... things had been so much pleasanter without him. But that was years ago. Funny that he should remember her – and even seem jovial, though he was clearly surprised and perhaps even put out.

"Do you normally carry on like this then, Liam?" Yes, that was his name... Liam Hutson. He had been half the size then, but still scraggy and undernourished. No mum or dad ever showed up for parents' evening. Of course, he'd lived with his nana.

By the time he was fifteen he had more or less stopped attending school. The only thing he'd ever wanted to talk about was his dog, Winston, that he'd rescued. The local paper had run a story about him: "Brave boy dives into dock to rescue mutt".

"No Miss," he said, still giving this crestfallen grin, the sort of expression you might have if you'd committed a small blunder.

"I should hope you don't."

"No, straight up, I don't."

"So why did you then?" Eleanor knew very little about young people and drug-taking, but she'd got the impression that most were up to some sort of drug fiddle and she suspected this must be the case here. No point in asking him – he would just deny it anyway.

"Needed money for a sandwich."

"I'm sure you did," she said, giving him her teacher's stern gaze, but with a twitch of her lips. She wanted to roar with laughter, double up with relief because she was still alive, and this character, Liam Hutson, the bane of her life, who always spelled 'where' 'were' and wrote 'I' with a small letter and said 'we was' should have been the attempted mugger. "You mean, you wanted it for your pills or whatever it is you're imbibing."

He did have the grace then to look embarrassed but his smile widened and he hauled up his hood.

Eleanor noticed that they had both been turned into snow people. "Well," she said, "if I ever see you in town, I'll buy you a sandwich and we'll have a chat maybe."

"Yes, Miss," he said, finally mounting his bike and riding off into the white gloom. It occurred to her then that she did have a cheese and pickle sandwich jammed down in her bag that she'd bought to eat but hadn't had time to. Pity she hadn't thought of that earlier.

THE CAROL SERVICE

I shall be very glad when this afternoon is over, though I suppose my being awake half the night hasn't improved things anyway. Chris, of course, never has any problem about sleeping. I was glad he kept to his side of the bed… I don't want to think about him – there are enough problems here without that.

"You are always so holier than thou," he said. "So sanctimonious. You're never wrong, ever."

If I can just get a few minutes alone before anybody comes into the chapel.

I'll start them with the Lord's Prayer – and I'll get them to remain standing, that way I shall be able to see if they start messing about. I've got to get a grip on things. If they sense you're not in control, you've lost it, and I can't afford that with Security breathing down my neck.

Why is it so cold in here? I can't stop shivering. Those workmen were supposed to have mended the heating system but I suppose it's like everything else here, it doesn't work. Even that poor crib looks as though it's been in an earthquake and Joseph needs a new nose. At least they can't see that the ox only has three legs. I probably shouldn't leave the wise men on that table – something's bound to happen to them. Then again, maybe I'll just have to chance it.

"Riots always kick off in the chapel, you know," the Security chap said, and he gave me that very cold clear stare. "You know what happened at Strangeways?"

"Oh yes," I said, "I'm quite well apprised of that."

His lip seemed to curl. "You can't have all those men in the chapel. It's a security risk."

That seems to be the new buzz word 'security', 'security risk'. Nothing else really matters. He wanted me to feel that the chaplaincy is just a frill, that we don't matter. I think they'd be pleased if something did kick off. You don't seem to understand, I said, these men have a right to come and worship… He looked at me as though I were mad. His cold blue eyes, shaven head and the sort of body that forces you to notice – he must have spent hours in the gym – all emphasised his brutal aura. I feel as though I'm caught in the middle of something… Where is God in all this?

I nod and smile at Marion as she sits down at the keyboard. At least she's ready for the influx – I wish I were. For people like Marion it must be so restful to believe that you've got a direct line to God and that He'll find you a place on the over-full car park and shield you from all riots.

No more chance of a moment alone. Here come the colleagues. I'm glad they're positioning themselves round the walls, that way they'll be able to keep a look out at what's happening.

This is it! The door to the chapel bangs back and in they come, muttering and spluttering with laughter. Their eyes are everywhere. The one straddling a seat, after executing several gymnastic manoeuvres, lands down miraculously three rows in front. Another chap scrambles onto a chair seat in order to hop a row and reach his mates. I have to stop myself from telling him to remember other people have to sit on those seats – no wonder everything in here looks so battered. They jostle one another and spray everywhere with curses. No change there.

I wish we could get started. Three wings are in now by my count, still one more to come. Slack times like this are when things can blow up. I shouldn't have put my vest on after all, I'm starting to sweat.

Peter Squires is sitting two rows back with his head in his hands. It's only two days since he heard that his baby had died. "Why did God let it happen?" he said. I had to fight an impulse to give him a hug... I couldn't trot out easy platitudes. Darren Summers has a strained look round his eyes. "My Mam's been sectioned," he said and the tears were running down his face. "It's all my fault..." And there's Mal Chambers whose partner's left him and who says she'll not let him see his children again because he's a druggy.

I wonder how we're going to get through the next hour and a half. They're manic because they've been let out and there's a chance to natter with someone from another wing... this is when something could kick off. Don't forget Strangeways. And that look from the Security man... The three prison officers just stare straight ahead of them.

At last they've arrived! A lot of these chaps will be the twenty-three hours a day bang-up ones, those who don't work or go on education. They make for the back rows, dragging their feet in unlaced prison sandshoes. Then Glen Williams swaggers in wearing his expensive trainers. No maroon prison sweat shirt for him, he's showing off his muscles in a black vest. He's told me proudly that he's a 'heavy', in other words an extortionist, who visits drug addicts who haven't paid for their drugs on time. Oh God, here come Wayne Slyte and mate, Baz. They shunt themselves into the middle of the row next to the back one and grin round inanely and a gust of laughter snags along the rows nearby. This spells trouble. Slyte can disrupt a Bible study group in a fraction of a second. Some chaplains have banned him because he is so disruptive and annoying. I expect he's gone through life so far being a nuisance and being ejected from places. I don't need this.

I take a deep breath and move forward. "Welcome to our carol service," I hear myself say, "and of course this is my first service in the prison. I hope you will all help to make it a time of reverence and joy." Chattering splinters the silence. I ask them all to stand and tell them we are going to pray. "Our Father who art in heaven," I start. I daren't close my eyes but keep them lowered so that I can see what's going on in front of me. Their voices grunt along more or less keeping pace with mine but I can hear Slyte puttering on in a falsetto. He is clearly trying to send the prayer up. I feel my face growing hot with rage. My heart thumps – I'm back in yesterday evening with Chris yelling at me. "When have you ever been wrong, Ruth? Does it ever occur to you that living with such a holier than thou creature is tiring?" There were other things too... awful things. All because I said he should show some Christian tolerance towards his mother.

"We are now going to sing Oh Little Town of Bethlehem." A general shuffling about follows whilst some say they can't find the page or it isn't in their carol sheets or they've got different sheets. Just the usual palaver. Marian strikes up on the keyboard. The first few rows seem to be singing all right but Slyte and co at the back chanter on as a raucous counterpoint. I can't see him at all and I realise that he must have draped himself over the seats so that I can't observe what he's getting up to.

Bill gives a rendering of the first lesson in his hearty Methodist way, though interruptions rumble on the back two rows. Will I bring everything to a halt and bawl Slyte out or shall I pretend I'm unaware of what he's doing? He obviously wants to draw attention to himself and if I refuse to gratify his need, perhaps he'll pipe down. But he might not, and if he has to be hauled out by prison officers, I will have abdicated my authority. No, I've got to keep going. We shall be all right during the carols. It's a pity there isn't a massive organ to drown out Slyte and co.

They're up for Once in Royal David's City. Still no sign of Slyte, he'll be making a point by sprawling on the seats. The row in front of him keep turning round and grinning.

Alan reads the next lesson. He doesn't approve of women priests. I can see Slyte has draped himself across two seats. Sister Benedicta sends him a stern look but he appears to take no notice.

DAPHNE GLAZER

IIIIIIIIIIIIIIIIIIIIIIIIIIIIIIIIIIIIIIIIIIIIIIIIIIIIIIIIIIIIIIIIIIIIIIIIIIIIIIIIIIIIIIIIIIIIIIIIIIIIIIIIIIIIIIIIIIIIIIIIIIIIIIIIIIIIIIIIIIIIIIIIIIIIIIIIIIIIIIIIIIIIIIIIIIIIIIIIIIII

They all stagger up scraping their chairs on the parquet for In the Bleak Midwinter. The singing sounds raucous and stringy – perhaps they don't know this carol. I'm sweating as they plough through the verses. I just wish Marion could play on indefinitely so that I won't have to give my address. Then I'm up and looking into their faces – if I maintain eye contact I might succeed in quelling them. I meet Slyte's pale eyes. He smiles. I pretend I haven't seen him and I move into my theme: the Light.

"Which is more important," I say, "the sun or the moon?"

"The Sun!" Slyte chirps up.

"Nice one, Slytie," Glen Williams oozes from the row behind.

"Show respect!" an older man says.

"Go on then, Ruth, you haven't answered me," Slyte persists.

"Now if we say only the Sun is important, we are making a big mistake."

Slyte wants to argue and comes on again. I flounder on about darkness being essential or we will not be able to see the Light, then, thankfully I focus on Jesus being 'the Light of the world.'

"We all have to try to let the Light radiate from us."

While I struggle on I can hear a constant rumble from the Slyte row. Keep going, keep going, nearly through – but I shan't let them get away with it.

"Right," I say gazing into their faces, "are you letting the Light radiate from you? The fact that so many of you are in prison would indicate that you are not doing so. This is a time for taking stock."

"This dun't make us feel very cheerful – not very good at Christmas," Slyte shouts.

"Well it's not meant to," I say. I can feel water draining down my armpits. "We all have to examine uncomfortable things about ourselves and our behaviour from time to time. You have to decide, by next Christmas will you still be reacting in the same way to life, still set on coming back to prison."

At last it's time to sing the last carol. They bumble up again for Hark the Herald Angels Sing, except of course for Slyte and Baz.

"May the peace of God that passes all understanding keep your hearts and minds, amen," I say.

They begin to file out to the adjoining room for coffee and mince pies. I'm not going to let Slyte escape. I stand waiting as the others leave.

"Wayne, would you mind staying behind for a few minutes, please?" He gives a stupid grin, egged on by Baz.

"See, she fancies you," Baz says.

"That's quite enough, Baz, thank you," I say. "I don't need you as well."

Baz looks at Slyte.

"Come here, Bazy." Slyte instructs but the call of mince pies proves stronger and Baz disappears. The chapel door swings shut.

My heart bangs. Rage makes my hands shake. "Well," I say, forcing him to meet my eyes. His stupid grin slips. "I have found your behaviour most upsetting, Wayne. Can you imagine what it's like for me? Here I am, my first Christmas as a chaplain in prison and you try to ruin the service."

His gaze drops. "I didn't mean to like."

"But can't you see what it's like? Calling out? Interrupting – I needed your support – why did you do it?"

He shifts his trainers about and looks blank.

"Well?" I wait. Right through the service I wanted to scream at him, beat him to pulp. By the time I'd reached the blessing I thought I'd burst.

"I dunno."

"I think you've got into a habit of trying to draw attention to yourself, Wayne, and believe me, it is tedious." I can see he has nothing more to say. "I shall have to ban you from all chapel groups."

"Don't ban us, Ruth."

The sight of his pale pinched face halts me. It's the face of a little kid, somebody who's never got the treats, always been ignored. I hesitate.

"All right," I say at last, "but in future please get a grip on yourself. Go and get a mince pie before they've all gone."

"Sorry," he mutters. He meets my eye now and we both smile.

Afterwards when they've all been taken back to the wings and we're carrying trays of dirty crockery into the kitchen where the washing up is underway, I moan on about Slyte. Sister Benedicta is beside me wiping crumbs into a plastic refuse bag.

"That boy is such a mixture – always in prison, but do you know I read in the evening paper last year, he jumped into the dock and saved this child from drowning. They gave him an award," Sister Benedicta says. "We're all such a mixture of things."

"Yes."

As I'm walking up the road towards the prison car park in the four o'clock gloom, I stare at the sky before me and on the horizon gleams of brightness fade into a rosy wash the colour of cherry blossom, and I'm humming.

THE VISIT

Friday morning. June. The heat on the Fours stifles. Not a wisp of air. Most of the tiny windows in the pads have been blocked up, except for a few holes. In pad 25 Gary Sharp lies on his back, four landings up under the burning roof panes, and stares at the ceiling. A few feet away his pad mate, Baz, a letter S, snores beneath a blanket.

On the landing outside the screw bellows, mustering the crew for the workshops. Cons yell back and forth; trainers grate on metal stairs. Way beyond the perimeter wall lorries thunder on the road, and out on the estuary a ship wails.

Sweat pools at the base of his throat and starts out from under his hairline.

He imagines standing under a cold shower with the jets of water drumming on his skull and trickling down his shoulder blades.

You can visualize anything in here – throw your mind into places where your body can't go and for a while it's as though you're there – but then you land back in the pad and the disappointment pains and your mouth fills with sourness. But today, this afternoon, Kimberly will visit – well, she might. You can't tell with her. No point banking on it, that way lies disaster. You learn one thing pretty fast in nicks, and that is; let go. The way to survive is: hang loose; stay free. Girls come, girls go. He glances across at Baz. Of course Baz is only in his twenties, a while before he'll have learned the lesson, and so he tortures himself thinking about his girlfriend and who's bedding her.

"You don't miss a slice off of a sliced loaf," Gary tells him. But Baz always pulls a face and says Gary doesn't understand, what about his kids?

But Gary does understand, knows it too well. Of course you tend to forget how it once was – no, perhaps not 'forget', just refuse to acknowledge. Because you have to save yourself in the end.

Of course you can float along in the nick. Gary has perfected the art. If you stay on 'basic', which means twenty-three hour a day bang-up, no privileges, nothing, you can dream your way through blocks of days. Sometimes you get the chance of a bit of gear; things pass on the wings. Let them try all their might with MDTs, it'll still happen – and anyway, if you're on basic, there's nothing to lose: no TVs, no association. They've taken everything off of you, so from that position, you're free, you're strong… and of course there's the other lads, same old faces, barring the ones who've not made it; those who've OD-ed, and you've known plenty of them. They follow a pattern. In the nick they work, get moved to an enhanced, drug-free wing, have a telly in their cells: the reward, the carrot. Oh yes, they swear that on the out, they'll turn their backs on the dreaded smack. They've given up for good. No weakening. That's it.

Going to live the life of the righteous citizen, work, have a wife and kids and a dog and a mortgage – or a council house on a better estate. They're young kids… there was Jasey last week. The wing hummed with it. Always the same… a death and everybody wants to know the details, but then they shrug their shoulders. So? Jasey left nick, a mate met him at the gate.

Just have one hit, mate, they said. Jasey did, and it killed him. Found dead in his mam's front room.

Oh, he'd given up, his mam said, wasn't doing drugs no more… it's a scandal.

Newspaper pictures of grieving mam and dad. They stare at the camera with lumpy faces and dead-cod eyes, say they did their best, couldn't stop him, didn't know he was at it.

Looking at it squarely, you could say that the kids who swear they'll not touch smack again, have given up, are just plain weak. They're never going to make it anyway. In their hearts they know it's got them: it's a craving, a crazy desire and there's no use denying it, smack is the irresistible woman who seduces you. You'll not shake it off, not ever. When you've got a rattle on, you'd kill for it, nothing on earth can hold you back.

Kimberley, if she comes, will sit there facing him across the table and he'll breathe in her scent and close his eyes for a heart beat. You get to long for the smell of shampooed hair and clean skin pliant with youth and moisturiser and the feel of a woman's mouth. You never see or touch wholesomeness in here… never. Basic is basic. You have to forget there can be anything else because it's part of the survival package.

The screws are unlocking for exercise. Gary gets out of bed, approaches the sink and runs the water.

"Come on, time to rise and shine."

Baz grunts and turns over.

"Get your kegs on!"

"What?"

"Exercise."

Outside, wind smelling of kippers bounces in their faces. The sun blazes. A blackbird sings perched on a billow of razor wire. Gary looks up and something inside him hurts. He won't examine it – not now, not later. He exchanges a few words of news with a couple of lads and they laugh. The sun makes him blink. It washes the tarmac with brightness. You get to believe that nothing else exists except this Victorian fortress. They used to top guys in here – he's heard the hanging cell is on D Wing. Ones and now YPs will be installed there, never knowing what vibes must be oozing from the walls of their pad.

Later when he collects his metal tray with soggy chips plonked on it and the pan-scrubber fish-cake and mushy peas, he notices his stomach muscles have clenched. It makes you gag, that and the smell of sweaty bodies and feet. On such days the place seems too tight for them all.

Baz is uneasy. His partner's coming for a visit. "If she's going with that bastard, I'll do him."

"You don't know and you don't want to know," Gary tells him. "It's no skin off of your nose. By the time you get out, she'll have got tired of him anyway."

"So you think she is then?"

"What?"

"Is going with him?"

"Chill man!"

Baz's wittering prevents him thinking, and before he knows it, he's in the visits' hall, with the stupid red plastic bib on that all cons have to wear for visits, and looking at the red plastic tables and chairs that are bolted to the ground.

He's sitting waiting when a woman saunters in. Bleached hair swings against cheeks that are pale as milk. He remembers the wide cheek bones and the pouty lips. Eighteen years since he saw. The cheek bones have sharpened and several bold lines incise the forehead and mouth. But it's a handsome, sexy face. It stirs something inside him like the blackbird did, singing its heart out on the wire. She looks directly at him. He stares back and wants to speak but can't, because she moves away to another table. He follows the sway of her buttocks under the tight, knee-length skirt and her bare legs and feet in their stiletto-heeled sling-backs. He would like to run his fingers down those pale legs. He must know why she's there. He feels the sweat beading on his forehead. It will be worse for him if he knows the guy she's come to visit.

Baz natters with his girlfriend while their kids swarm on the chairs. Gary wonders how the visit's going.

Kimberly clops in, wiggling her pelvis so that the lads will take notice. He smiles across at her. A gust of her scent hits his nostrils.

"Phew," she says, sitting down opposite him. "Innit hot?" She's wearing a bright pink vest with tiny straps that fall off one shoulder.

"How've you been then, Kim?" he says, and tries to concentrate on her, though he's really intent on seeing what the woman at the other table is doing. She has sat down and faces a blond, well-set up kid, though Gary can only see the back of his head and his shoulders.

"Do you like me new top then?" Kimberly says. "You don't seem that impressed."

"Oh yer... I am, love..." He takes her hands, leans across and kisses her, thrusting his tongue between her lips, searching the hot, wet place beyond. They part, gasping, and she sits back settling her shoulder straps and preens. He can taste her lipstick.

He catches the eye of the blond woman two tables away. She holds his gaze and doesn't smile. He isn't sure what he reads there. Kimberley's conversation hops about. She's busy decorating. Some kid has had his car fire-bombed; somebody else got mugged. He keeps missing stuff, because he wants to exchange glances with the woman. She holds out on him; dodges; gazes down the hall; sneaks over his shoulder; refuses to be pinned down. He sweats.

"Did you hear what I said, Gary?"

"What? Yer... 'course."

"You all right?"

"Yer, fine... just the heat... it's that hot in the pad, it fries you!"

"Oh right... so I said to our Trace, shall we book for Ibiza and she said go for it... so we are."

"Good one!" He pictures Kimberley and her sister, Tracey, being wowed by the waiters... perhaps they won't come back. "You'll have to send us a card."

"You bet," she says, and pouts.

He burns with impatience to know about the woman and who the young prisoner is.

"Sure you're all right, Gary?"

"Course I am."

He kisses her some more and holds her across the table, but his eyes still seek out the blond woman.

"Who're you staring at?" Kimberley cranes round to see. "Do you know her or sommat?"

"I used to be married to her," he says, unable to help himself. "A long time ago."

"You fancy her or sommat?"

"No way, nothing like that."

"Who's that kid she's with?"

"Dunno."

Time's up. Kimberley gives him a dramatic kiss and makes to toddle off. "Love you… take care, mind how you go," she says.

Gary barks with laughter. "And you take care, Kim – no need to bother about me. I'm well taken care of in here."

As the blond woman leaves, she darts a direct glance at him. The YP swivels round, and Gary sees his own face gazing back, and is immobilized with shock. Now he knows – this is his son, last seen when he was a few months old. The lad's face is blank because of course he has no idea that Gary is his father and Gary won't tell him. His mother obviously doesn't want the lad to know.

Now the move back onto the wing has started. Regret pierces him. Seventeen years ago he had a wife and son – and then he started shooting up and Sally left him. And that boy, his son, is headed out on the same road.

Back on the wing it's all like it was before, except it isn't. Gary stares round and lets his eyes rove the cell block to the glassed-in roof far above, with its painted-out panes. The heat hangs steady. Baz chatters on about how everything seems all right but you can't be sure and maybe she's having it off and what he'll do, if she is.

He knows something in his gut has to change, and it is as though a skin of indifference is being sloughed off him. He shivers in the heat, thinking of Sally with the pale face and shiny legs, and his son, that tall blond boy on the threshold of adulthood, and the tears burn at the back of his throat.